"Fed me a pack of lies, didn't you?"

Terri shook her head. "You are mistaken. I told no lie."

"Miss Divine, we're not playing a game. You conned me out of a vast sum of money. There are laws against con games."

She gave a start. "Mr. Denton, I did not con you. You offered of your own free will to pay me..."

"For breaking an engagement that didn't exist in the first place."

Terri drew herself up. "The payment was for a promise not to marry Robert Goodrich. I am honoring that promise."

"You didn't intend to marry him in the first place!"

Dear Reader,

Help us celebrate life, love and happy-ever-afters with our great new series.

Everybody loves a party, and birthday parties best of all, so join some of your favorite authors and celebrate in style with seven fantastic new romances. One for every day of the week, in fact, and each featuring a truly wonderful woman whose story fits the lines of the old rhyme "Monday's child is..."

> Monday's child is fair of face
> Tuesday's child is full of grace,
> Wednesday's child is full of woe,
> Thursday's child has far to go,
> Friday's child is loving and giving,
> Saturday's child works hard for its living,
> And a child that's born on a Sunday
> Is bonny and blithe and good and gay.

(Anon.)

Does the day that you're born on affect your character? Some people think so—if you want to find out more, read our exciting new series. Available wherever Harlequin books are sold:

Happy reading,

The Editors, Harlequin Romance

Private Dancer
Eva Rutland

Harlequin Books

TORONTO • NEW YORK • LONDON
AMSTERDAM • PARIS • SYDNEY • HAMBURG
STOCKHOLM • ATHENS • TOKYO • MILAN
MADRID • WARSAW • BUDAPEST • AUCKLAND

ISBN 0-373-03412-1

PRIVATE DANCER

First North American Publication 1996.

CHAPTER ONE

THE belly dancer wore the usual trappings, the soft shimmery sheer folds of a harem costume, midriff bare between halter top and billowy pants suspended from the jeweled belt surrounding her pelvis. Same sensuous movements from the swing of her long black hair to the feathery tap of tiny bare feet.

Same trappings. Same erotic routine...but done with a certain delicacy. So exquisitely graceful, every gesture beautifully coordinated with the rhythmic click of the sils on her fingers.

Same... No. Different. Something set her apart. That was it. Apart. Fresh, untouched, remote...physically here, but not really present in Spike O'Malley's crowded, smoke-filled bar.

Mark Denton had chosen the table nearest the small circular stage, meaning to get a good look at her, size her up before he approached her. Now he leaned forward in his chair, completely enthralled, oblivious to everything but the captivating figure on the stage, the teasing come-play-with-me invitation in those slanting blue eyes. The provocative sway of her torso that evoked a hungry stirring in his groin. Damn! He sat up and took a hasty swallow of his Scotch. Forced himself to remember his uncle's words.

"A gold-digging slut! She's got her hooks into that damn fool grandson of mine who's ripe for the plucking."

"Can't pluck much, Uncle Jasper." Mark knew the old man kept a tight hold on the Goodrich millions. Tight hold on Robbie too. Time the boy cut loose. "Robbie's a good kid," he said. "He's entitled to a few wild oats."

"Wild oats I might countenance. Not marriage!"

This got Mark's attention. "Marriage!"

"That's his damn fool intention. And I won't have it!" Jasper Goodrich slapped a hand on his massive rosewood desk. "Not to some floozy who bobs her boobs and wiggles her belly in a bar full of goggle-eyed, beer-guzzling lechers."

Mark's lips twitched. "Personal inspection, Uncle?"

"Not on your life. Wouldn't be caught dead in such a place. It's called Spike's. And she is..." He searched among several papers. "Deedee Divine," he snorted. "Name ought to tell him she's a designing hussy. Robbie's a fool. But he's twenty. Old enough to pull off this damn fool stunt. I want you to put a stop to it."

"Me?"

"You're the syndicated columnist. Good with words. You know how to sway people to your way of thinking."

"Look, Uncle, I only report the facts. I don't—"

"Whatever." Jasper waved a hand as if to brush away any dissension. "The facts are that

Robbie's in deep. You've got to pull him out of this, Mark.''

Mark wasn't surprised. He was ten years older than Robbie, but the nearest to his age in the family and his appointed guardian since his birth. "I'll talk to him if you like. But I doubt it will do any good."

"It won't. Talk to the floozy."

"I don't even know the woman."

"No need to get acquainted. Your calling card will be cash in hand."

This shouldn't have surprised him either. According to Jasper Goodrich, it was money that made the world go around, and that was what he used to chart its course. Mark thought of his cousin, Janine. Money had broken up her impromptu marriage to that race car driver. The guy must have been the creep Jasper claimed, for, threatened with Janine's disinheritance, he had taken a pay off and run. Not that it did him much good. He had died in a crash soon after. And Mark's mother always said Janine had died more from a broken heart than from the ordeal of Robbie's birth. His Uncle Jasper had been devastated. Still, Mark mused, he evidently hadn't learned anything. Now he planned to use money to direct Robbie's life.

"Look, Uncle Jasper, maybe you're going about this the wrong way."

The older man was not to be deterred. "It's the only way, Mark. Make it clear to the gold digger that Robbie won't get one red cent if he marries her. I guarantee she'll come around. You can go up to half a million. And keep me out of it, understand? I don't want Robbie to know I've even talked to you."

That was why he has appealed to me instead of his battery of lawyers. At least he learned one thing from his experience with Janine. She had never forgiven him. He meant to hold on to Robbie's love. Leaving the dirty work to someone else.

"I'd rather not be involved, sir."

"You won't be, if you handle things right. Robbie's back east this week for a debating session. Talk to her while he's gone and tell her to keep her mouth shut. Now, don't be obstinate, Mark. You're not harming Robbie. You're keeping him from ruining his life! Do you want to see him tied up with a woman like that?"

"You're judging her sight unseen. Maybe she really cares for Rob."

"Ha! All she sees are dollar signs. If you don't believe me... try her!"

So Mark found himself consenting to his uncle's plan. Robbie was young, impulsive. It wouldn't hurt to take an objective look at the woman, put her to the test.

Put her to the test. That was why he was here. He wrenched himself from the euphoric trance and tried to observe her with a cold detachment. The dance ended and he watched her retreat to an echo of cheers and clapping hands. Watched her return to blow kisses to her audience. Observed her eyes. That teasing come-play-with-me glint was gone, replaced by a hard, cold glow.

Uncle Jasper could be right. Her eyes held an almost unholy gleam. Greed? More than greed...a wild, reckless hunger. More. A firm determination to get whatever she hungered for.

The unholy gleam was a wild conglomeration.

Elation! Aunt Meg's blood matched. She could be a donor for Mom.

Desperation. Where could she get three hundred and fifty thousand dollars for a bone marrow transplant?

Determination. Mom's life was at stake. She would get it. But where? Dear God, where?

The agonizing thoughts riveted through Terri Thompson's brain as she automatically clicked her sils, pivoted on her toes and wriggled her torso. She loved to dance, and usually every disturbing problem was blocked out as she did so.

But not this one.

The dance ended to a thundering crescendo of applause and she ran from the stage. Straight into the massive bulk of Spike O'Malley. His cigar dangled through tobacco-stained teeth as he grinned at her.

"You're great, kid! Better'n your mom. Listen to them dudes. Better take another bow," he urged, giving her a push.

She took the bow, but shook her head to the calls for another rendition, blew kisses with both hands and again sped from the stage. She had to get away. To think. She evaded Spike O'Malley's open arms, but gave him a warm smile as she disappeared into the dressing room. The bar owner was a kind, warmhearted man, and it was good of him to allow her to take her mother's place. Her weekly four-night stint in the bar more than doubled her State job paycheck.

But it wasn't enough. A ball of fear knotted in her stomach. She drew a deep breath. Relax. Whatsoever you believe in your mind...

"How is Deedee doing, kid?" Vashti, the curvaceous blonde waitress, looked up from one of the chairs, genuine concern in her hazel eyes.

"Much better." Never admit a negative thought! Anyway, things were positive. The cancer had not spread. The myeloma was confined strictly to the bones. If she got a bone marrow transplant... She straightened, tightened her mouth. Not if! When she got the transplant!

Three hundred and fifty thousand dollars! On top of everything else. She was working two jobs and she had not yet covered the cost of the hospital and all those tests.

Again she heard the doctor's voice. "Her only hope of recovery. But, bone marrow transplants are still experimental, you see, and therefore, noninsurable."

Noninsurable! She felt a burst of indignation. All these years Mom had paid the premiums for insurance, which only covered eighty percent of the monstrous cost of the hospital and tests just to determine what she had. And nothing to affect a cure! This wasn't right. Everybody was entitled to proper health care, and she hoped somebody would do something to guarantee it. Even so, it would be too late for Mom. If she didn't get—

"It was such a shock!" Vashti drew on her cigarette. "Deedee was the last person you'd expect to collapse like that. She was so...so alive. Always laughing and joking."

Yes, that was Mom, Terri thought. Her work as a dancer often kept her on the road, but her interludes at home were like a breath of fresh air for Terri. All music, dancing and laughter, as they practiced her routines.

"She was out there dancing as usual when all of a sudden she just flopped." Vashti shook her head. "I tell you, it scared the life out of me."

"Scared me, too." Terri had slipped out of her costume. Now she donned a white silk dress with a low neck, drop waistline and pleated miniskirt. "Show those legs," Spike had said.

"You sure got here in a hurry."

"I suppose. Seemed like hours to me." She had wasted no time after getting Spike's phone call. Her mother had pulled out of what they thought was a faint when she got there. But she had looked so pale, Terri had decided it was Deedee's last night at work. It was time for her to take care of Mom. This she proceeded to do, taking her first for a thorough checkup. That was when they found that Deedee needed more than rest.

When the hospital bills began to mount, Terri remembered Spike's words. "Can you dance, kid? If your mom's going to be laid up for a while..."

Certainly she could do for Mom what Mom had done for her. It was fortunate that she was out of school and two months into her new job at California's State Commission on Economic Development. And fortunate that they were in the same area. It hadn't been that way for a long time, with Deedee working on the East Coast and Terri at Stanford University. When Terri's Master's in Business Adminstration had landed her the good job with the commission, they had been delighted.

Mom had come out to help her get settled in an apartment and decided to stay. "Think I'll try the West Coast circuit for a while." She had chortled. "So I can keep an eye on you." She had laughed when she said it. As if touring the circuit was fun...and not this, Terri thought as she looked around the tawdry dressing room. How was it she had never realized what it had cost her mother to care for Aunt Meg, herself and her two cousins?

Terri knew very little about her father, Terance Thompson. Only that he had been her mother's dancing partner and deserted her when Terri was two years old. Delia Thompson had never looked back. She had changed her name and her routine to become Deedee Divine, belly dancer. Her sister Meg, and husband, Jack, had taken over the care of Terri, along with their own two children. When Terri's beloved uncle Jack had died prematurely, Delia had insisted that Meg remain at home to care for the children.

"Can't stand latchkey kids," she said. "I'll support you." She had, until both Meg's daughters had become schoolteachers. And now that I'm off her back, this has to happen.

It must have been hard on her, supporting all of us, Terri thought as she brushed the long black hair on the wig that covered her own auburn curls. The wig was part of the costume that identified her as Deedee Divine, and she never removed it when she went out to sit with customers between shows. Part of Deedee's job, Spike had explained.

I took all she did for granted, never knowing what it cost. But how could she? She had never even seen her mother perform except when she was in one of those Broadway shows, and it had never occurred to her how seldom that was. She knew Mom had never made the big time, but not that she had been reduced to this.

"Yes, indeed, kid, you're doing just great."

With a start, Terri realized that Vashti had continued to talk to her. "Thank you," she said.

"Good you can take her place. Keep the cash flowing. Speaking of which, I'd better get going." Vashti snuffed out her cigarette. She stood and touched Terri's shoulder. "You can stay here as long as you like. Spike likes you. I can tell."

And that's another problem, Terri thought, as she watched Vashti depart. How long can I fend him off without offending? Not that it matters. Even this job won't bring in three hundred and fifty thousand dollars. A bone marrow transplant, the doctor had said, was her mother's only chance. That had given them hope. But when he added that she would have to go to a hospital in Seattle for the surgery and what it would cost,

Terri had been appalled. And scared. No way could they raise that kind of money.

"Pray," Aunt Meg had said. "Whatever you ask in prayer..."

"Visualize," Angie had advised. Angie, one of the clerks at Terri's State office, had some weird ideas. She insisted that if you kept seeing in your mind whatever you wanted to happen, it would really happen. "Try it," she told Terri. "It really works."

Terri was desperate enough to try everything. She prayed, visualized and racked her brain for some way...

Whatever you see in your mind... She reminded herself that three days ago they hadn't had a donor. When her own blood hadn't matched, she had phoned Aunt Meg and asked her to come out. She had shut her eyes, seeing Meg here, hearing her say, "I match. I match. I can be a donor. After all your mother has done for me..."

And today, just today, she had heard Aunt Meg say almost those very words.

Whatsoever you believe in your mind... She shut her eyes, saw herself smiling at the doctor, counting out crisp new thousand-dollar bills.

Keeping the vision in mind, she slipped on her pumps and moved toward the door. Once in the bar, she glanced around, hoping to see some of the college boys from Berkeley. They were nice young men whose company she much preferred to the more aggressive customers. They would continue to buy drinks to keep her at their table.

None of them were there, and she remembered that Robbie had said he would be away this week. Also, he was very upset with her. But she really had thought it a joke when they talked about getting married. She knew he had become attached to her. Since that night he had gotten stinking drunk and she had taken him home with her, not wanting him to drive in his condition. He had slept it off on her sofa. She had given him coffee and a hearty breakfast next morning and sent him on his way. He still came often to the bar and they had become good friends. Since the night of his binge, they had devised a way of dumping the excess drinks into a nearby planter, keeping them sober while the drinks kept coming and she remained at his table. She really enjoyed him, but had thought the marriage idea a joke until the other night when he tried to present her with an honest-to-goodness real diamond engagement ring.

"But, Robbie, I thought you were joking," she had said.

He looked stunned. "Joking? About marriage?"

"Well, we've been kidding around about so many things. But, Robbie, marriage is a serious business and you're much too young to—" She broke off, knowing she had said the wrong thing.

"So you're just like everybody else! You think I'm too young to know my own mind."

"No. I didn't mean that. It's... Well..." She hesitated, not wanting to hurt him. "Marriage is just not possible for me right now. And you...the truth is you're young, Robbie, and you need to wait. Meet others, widen your horizon, so to speak.''

"The truth is that while I'm making all kinds of plans to marry you and take you out of this dump, you've been just stringing me along. Isn't that it?''

She had tried to placate him, but he had left in a huff. Maybe he wouldn't be back at all. And maybe that was just as well. She certainly had no intention of marrying him, and the less he saw of her, the sooner he'd get over his infatuation.

She took another quick look around. None of the Berkeley boys were there tonight. Her heart sank as she heard the calls throughout the room.

"Over here, babe!''

"What's your pleasure, kid?''

Then she heard a quiet cultivated voice behind her. "Miss Divine?''

"Yes,'' she said, turning. A man she had never seen before was looking at her. He was tall, rather handsome, with black hair and dark, deep set eyes that seemed to be boring into her.

"Would you join me?'' he asked, motioning toward a secluded table. "There's a little matter I'd like to discuss with you.''

CHAPTER TWO

HE LED her to the secluded booth, instinctively feeling a need to protect her. To shield her. From what? She was a regular here, wasn't she? And yet, he again sensed a remoteness about her. He wasn't sure why. She had walked in with graceful dignity, head high, as if perfectly at ease in these surroundings. But in that simple white dress, her long black hair hanging to her waist, she had a look of purity and innocence. And, if her smile was a bit wary, it was also warm with such gracious sweetness that for a moment he felt a stab of pure envy. Robbie had seen her first.

God! He'd better get hold of himself.

He was aware of suspicious glances from several men. As if they too, felt the same instinct to protect her. From him, for Christ's sake! It made him nervous.

"It might be better," he suggested, even as they took their seats, "if we conducted this discussion elsewhere."

Her eyes widened, whether with surprise or mistrust he could not determine. "Sorry. I have less than an hour before my next performance."

"What I wish to say is rather private. Perhaps we could arrange a different time and place. I could call at your home, or, if you prefer, we could meet at—"

17

"No! I don't socialize with customers outside of business hours." It was definitely mistrust that surfaced now, and that irritated him. Business hours, indeed!

He was also irritated by the immediate appearance of a cocktail waitress with a bottle of champagne encased in a bucket of ice. Weren't they to have any privacy? "I didn't order that!" he snapped, starting to wave her away. Then he heard Miss Divine give a little cough and caught himself. "But perhaps Ms Divine . . . ?" He gave her a questioning look.

"Yes. My usual," she said, and nodded at the waitress. "Thank you, Vashti." She waited until drinks were poured and the waitress moved away. Then almost apologetically, she said, "During business hours they like me to socialize with customers who are drinking."

He gritted his teeth. This was a clip joint if he ever saw one, and she was part of the business! And making no bones about it!

Okay. So he needn't pull any punches. "I understand my nephew is one of your regular drinking customers."

She shrugged.

"I also understand that you have formed a rather close relationship with him."

"Oh?"

"One that extends beyond business hours," he added.

"You are mistaken." Defiance registered in those very expressive eyes. "I do not fraternize with customers away from these premises."

"Not even with a fiancé?"

"What are you talking about?"

"I am speaking of Robert Goodrich, the young man to whom you are engaged."

"I am not engaged to—" She stopped as understanding dawned. Robert Goodrich. Robert...Robbie. His nephew. This arrogant man was one of those pompous relatives Robbie was always griping about. Who told him he was a knucklehead who didn't know the time of day and was incapable of making any rational decision. They had really done a job on him, completely shattering his self-confidence. Old fogies, she had thought...grandfather, great-aunt? But this smooth-talking man in the well-cut business suit couldn't be much over thirty. He ought to know better than to treat Robbie like a child.

"You are...?" she inquired.

"Denton, Mark Denton. As I said, I'm Robbie's uncle and I am here to speak on his behalf."

"Oh? I think Robbie quite capable of speaking for himself."

His eyes narrowed. "In certain instances, perhaps. But marriage is a major step and wiser counsel should prevail."

Marriage? So Robbie hadn't told them of her rejection. Too hurt and embarrassed, poor kid.

"Robbie is young," he said. "Much too young to think of getting married."

"But well past the age of consent." She wouldn't betray Robbie. He could tell them in his own time and in his own way.

"True. But Robbie is young in more than years. I should think him hardly the type that would appeal to a woman of your..." He gestured as if searching for the right word. "A woman of...of your vast experience."

The implication stung. She knew what he thought of her. Okay! She'd play it to the hilt. "Guess you can't fight mother nature." She rolled her eyes expressively. "Every time Robbie just looks at me I get goose bumps all over," she said, adding under her breath, "take that, you stuffed shirt!"

He was watching her in amazement, or maybe it was disbelief. "Really, Miss Divine, that's hardly an indication of...of deep affection."

"Oh, but it is. First time I seen Robbie, him and me hit it off...just like that. Well...I guess you'd call it chemistry." She took a hasty swallow of champagne, almost choked but managed to turn it into a coy smile.

He glared at her. "It takes more than chemistry to sustain a marriage. I think you should know that Robbie's family is unalterably opposed to this union."

"Your problem, not mine!" Still seething, she looked around for a place to dump her drink. She couldn't dance if she drank more than—

"It might concern you that without family support, Robbie is virtually penniless."

"Oh?" She stared at him, suddenly tired of the game she was playing. Virtually penniless. That was her own status compared to what Mom needed. Dear God, what was she going to do?

Neither she nor her cousins had been working long enough to borrow even if any credit union would lend such a monstrous sum. No real property, and their savings were already exhausted. Her working two jobs didn't matter worth a darn. It wouldn't put a dent in what was needed. Three hundred and fifty thousand dollars. She sighed, feeling very tired.

"Aha! I see you are beginning to get my point." Terri was only vaguely aware that Denton was still talking. "Not only is Robbie now unemployed, but he has not yet finished school, has never worked a day in his life and has no money."

Terri, absorbed in her own thoughts, was not listening, but the last two words, which he emphasized, bounced out at her.

No money! No money! No! She mustn't think negative. "The money is there! We'll get it. Somehow we will!" She didn't realize she had spoken aloud, but Denton did. He sat up, put down his champagne glass with a clatter that brought her out of her reverie.

"I see Robbie has mentioned his ten-million-dollar trust fund!"

Terri's mouth opened. Ten million. Robbie had ten million dollars? He would lend her the money for Mom. She knew he would, whether she married him or not. Oh, God, where had he said he was going? She would get in touch with him and—

"Forget it! Robbie can't touch it. Jasper Goodrich set it up so that it's airtight. Robbie will not get it until he's thirty, and not then if he marries you. Understand?''

It was mind-boggling. Ten million dollars just sitting somewhere. Airtight. When all that was needed to keep Mom alive was a measly three hundred and fifty thousand. "It's not fair," she murmured, not realizing she spoke aloud. "Not fair."

"Fair or not, that's the way it is. And speaking of that, what about being fair to Robbie? Do you want him to lose his entire inheritance?''

"Lose it? What do you mean?''

"I mean that his grandfather has made it un-equivocally clear that if Robbie marries you, he will be cut off without a cent. His present allowance discontinued, the trust fund converted, everything gone...swish!" He waved a hand, emphasizing his point.

Terri was too stunned to speak. Her emotions jolted between anger and dismay. That anyone could be so dictatorial and diabolical! Suppose she and Robbie were really in love?

The man before her smiled and nodded. "I see you are beginning to understand. Now, think about this. Are you being fair to yourself?''

"Fair to myself?'' What was he talking about?

"Think about it. Under the circumstances, I think you will find Robbie, as a husband, more a burden than an asset. On the other hand—'' He was interrupted by the appearance of Vashti. He looked up in annoyance as Vashti poured, giving Terri a chance to dump the contents of her oversize champagne glass into the ice bucket. And

giving her a chance to think. Robbie was rich.
His family was so strongly opposed to his marrying her that he would lose everything if he did.
Robbie? Either he was being stubbornly independent or he hadn't had a chance to tell them
there was to be no marriage. So, unable to persuade him, they had come to her. She sighed.
Should she tell them or let Robbie—

"Now, Miss Divine, we are not without compassion." Vashti had disappeared, and Denton
was speaking to her with a kind of...sarcasm?
"The family is willing to compensate for your
loss."

"Compensate? My loss?"

"We realize that this is a painful decision for
you. But should you decide to release your hold
on Robbie, we would like to make you a gift
of...say, one hundred thousand dollars."

She gasped. One hundred thousand dollars for
doing what she wasn't going to do anyway! One
hundred thousand dollars! But, of course that
was just a drop in the bucket compared to ten
million...and that was just Robbie's share alone.
And they were willing to pay her, almost one third
of what she needed. But suppose she refused?
Her business acumen surfaced. She began to cal-
culate. If she played her cards right... She blinked
rapidly, hoping to squeeze out a few tears.

"I can't believe this. You're asking me to give
up Robbie...to forget what we have...for—for
money?" She put a hand to her mouth and
shook her head. "I couldn't...can't do that,"
she choked.

Mark Denton knew an act when he saw one. He had seen that calculating gleam in her eyes before she pulled this tearful maneuver. This woman was a pro at more than dancing. Damn! You sure couldn't judge a book by its cover. That cover of fresh, innocent beauty has Robbie hooked, lock, stock and barrel. Robbie? Hell, she almost had me going with all that sweetness and graciousness that seems to emanate from her. She's a dish, no doubt about it.

And Uncle Jasper was right. Nothing but hard, cold cash would pry this dish from Robbie. The question was, how much?

It worked! It really worked. Maybe praying and visualizing were the same thing. Thank you, God. And thank you, Angie. It worked. She had visualized herself counting out crisp thousand dollar bills and smiling, knowing that Mom was going to be all right. She didn't exactly have bills, but in her pocket was a check for four hundred thousand dollars. Not only would it pay for the surgery, it was enough to cover the cost of Mom and Aunt Meg's stay in Seattle, and probably six months of after-surgery therapy.

Terri felt a surge of relief. A heavy burden had been lifted from her. Like magic! So strange how it had come about. If she hadn't been dancing in Mom's place, if she hadn't met Robbie... That's the way it is, Angie had said. "You don't have to figure how it's going to happen. Just see it happening."

And that's what she had done. She had prayed and visualized—

You lied!

No. Not exactly. I couldn't help it if he thought...

You helped him think it!

All right! If God or somebody up there thought this was the way to get the money for Mom, I wasn't supposed to stand in the way, was I? Anyway, she promised, as guilt punctured the surge of relief, I'll pay it back. Every penny.

Ha! Four hundred thousand dollars!

People pay for houses and cars, don't they? In monthly payments. Okay, it may take me forever. But I will pay it back. I promise. I'll start paying as soon as I get Mom settled.

Terri worked in a hurry. She took off from work the next day and deposited the check. Before they could stop it, for some crazy reason...like hearing the truth from Robbie! But they wouldn't tell him they had paid her off, would they? No. Denton had not only made her promise not to marry Robbie, but also not to tell him that she and Denton had ever met.

Denton. Mark Denton. Last night the name had sounded familiar to her. And now in the clear light of day, she realized why. Mark Denton. His column was the first thing she read every morning in the *Chronicle*. He wrote about everything, politics, the economy, human events. Always, she had thought, he got to the heart of the problem, told it like it was. She had thought him so fair in his assessment of any issue, had begun to respect his opinions.

Not any more. Not after last night. Now she knew him for what he was. An arrogant, opinionated, conceited bastard who manipulated people with the written word. And with money!

Now why did she feel this wave of disappointment? Because when she had first seen him, she had thought... Well, what was she to think? He had such an honest, clean-cut look. A man to be trusted. Yes, his appearance was as straightforward as his editorials, but...

Oh, bother! Why was she thinking of him? No need to look a gift horse in the mouth. She notified her mother's doctor to schedule an immediate appointment at the Seattle hospital.

The difficulty was explaining to Mom and Aunt Meg.

"I got the money," she said. "A loan from a Mr Jasper Goodrich." She had made a note of the name and address on the check so she would know where to send her payments.

Delia Thompson stared at her daughter in astonishment. "Someone loaned you three hundred and fifty thousand dollars?"

"Four hundred thousand," said Terri.

"The Lord save us," Aunt Meg said. "He moves in a mysterious way, His wonders to perform. He plants His footsteps on the sea and rides upon the storm!"

But Delia Thompson was more worldly than her sister, and the look she turned upon Terri was incredulous and somewhat suspicious.

"Nobody in his right mind would lend you that much money."

"Isn't it amazing!" Terri said, knowing she would have to do some tall talking to convince her mother. Well, if she could put on an act for Denton, she could certainly put on one for Mom. "He's a philanthropist, you see, and likes to personally help someone who is in need."

"And just picked me out of the clear blue sky?" Delia, just home from the hospital, looked a little pale, but no one would dream she was deathly ill. No, not deathly. Terri knew the transplant would restore her to perfect health, and nothing was going to stop her getting it.

"The hospital, Mom! He heard about your case through the hospital and contacted me. A loan, not a gift." Terri thought rapidly. "He likes people to feel it's a business deal, not charity. They can pay back what he gives them in . . . their own time." She would pay it back. She would. She managed to talk so convincingly that Delia looked at her with astonishment.

"A remarkable man," she said. "And so kind. I'll write him a thank-you note."

"Do that," said Terri. "I'll mail it for you." One more lie. Once you got started you got tangled in a mess of them. Once back at the office, she told Angie the same lie she told her mother.

Angie wasn't surprised. "That's the way it works, Terri. You have this big problem, so big you can't imagine any way out. But the solution already exists. All you have to do is call it up.

Just like you call up a document on this computer.''

Terri shook her head. "Angie, you don't look like you're from out of space, but sometimes I believe—''

"Worked, didn't it?''

"Well, yes, but..." Terri was still filled with the wonder. "I would never have thought—''

"That's it. You don't think. You just tap into this computer." Angie tapped her head. "And call up whatever you want.''

"Maybe.'' Terri looked down at the sheaf of paperwork she had neglected while getting her mother off to Seattle. Applications for loans for small businesses—bookstore, dance school, pottery plant. People struggling on their own and needing a lift. But before they got a loan they had to prove what they could do. "People have to work for what they want,'' she said. "You can't just think up something and, presto! There it is.''

"You did it and your mom's on the way to Seattle, isn't she?''

Terri nodded dubiously, her practical mind still wrestling with the miracle of four hundred thousand dollars landing in her lap.

But there was nothing dubious about Angie. She perched on the edge of Terri's desk and pointed a convincing finger. "And listen to this. You know how fed up I've been with my puny little apartment on Beacon Street?'' Again Terri nodded. "Well, I just put what I wanted into my computer." Angie ran a hand through her sleek pixie haircut. "You have to be exact, you know. You don't just picture any old thing. Well, I decided I wanted one of those big condos on Coastal Green, you know, right off the park where they fly kites and you can sunbathe, and near the Coastal Yacht Club where most any day you could run into a most eligible bachelor, and—"

"Where you can't afford the rent, even if you could raise the down payment required for a lease," Terri finished.

"Oh, yeah? Listen to this. Marge Sims, in accounting, has just broken up with you-know-who, and consequently can no longer afford that big condo on guess where—Coastal Green. She's taking her broken heart to L.A. and needs someone to pick up her lease, no down, mind you. So there! Did I get what I programmed, or didn't I?"

"Uh-huh, I guess. But isn't the rent pretty steep?"

"I'm working on that." Angie shut her eyes as if visualizing and murmured, "A compatible roommate to share the cost...someone who won't borrow my clothes or steal my boyfriends, who—" Angie's eyes opened, focused on Terri. "You! You're too small for my clothes and too honest to make a grab for my friends. How about it, Terri?"

Terri hesitated. "I don't know..."

"Look, it's perfect for you, too. Your mom's going to be in Seattle for half a year or more. But there's that third bedroom, and wouldn't it be a beautiful setting for her to recuperate in? We could still share fifty-fifty.''

Not a bad idea, Terri decided. Her half would be more than she was paying for her two bedroom, but not that much more. And it might be a good time to move. She dreaded facing Robbie if he came back to the bar or to her apartment. He didn't know her name, and if she moved, it was likely she'd never see him again. She had given Spike notice, and had only one more week at the bar. Robbie was so mad with her, maybe he wouldn't show up. She hoped not. Even if he didn't know what she had done, she hated facing him. She cared what Robbie thought of her.

She didn't care what that stuffed shirt of an uncle of his thought! And she was glad she had taken the money.

Mark didn't care about the money. Jasper Goodrich had plenty of that, and if he wanted to wave it around like a baton directing people this way or that, that was his business!

But it always surprised him how easily people could be directed by money. That girl in Spike's Bar. She hadn't looked like she was starving or in dire need of anything. And there was something in her face, something that haunted, something familiar.

That poem, the one that had been in a frame on his mother's bedside table for as long as he could remember. "A womanly woman, who on every hand, sheds the luster of purity, goodness, and grace ... Who carries her loveliness stamped on her face."

That was it. Her face had goodness and grace stamped all over it. He had seen it in the way she smiled at those seedy men in the bar, gaining their respect. And the way she had looked at him, apologizing for that champagne...

Damn! He was at it again, completely befuddled by her. Forgetting the greed that had flashed in her eyes the minute he mentioned money. That had blown her cover, all right. Good thing he was more experienced at judging people than Robbie.

Robbie. Young, gullible, inexperienced ... and vulnerable. He'd never see beyond the cover, and wouldn't know about the payoff. When he learned the engagement was off, he was going to be hurt. Very hurt.

Mark didn't know what he could do or say to ward off Robbie's disappointment. But it was his concern for the boy that impelled him to meet Robbie's incoming plane. Maybe he could feel Robbie out, make some comments about Miss Deedee Divine that would in some way give a hint of what she really was.

He was at the gate when Robbie disembarked, and felt guilty at the bright smile that greeted him. "Mark! What the hell are you doing here?"

"Thought I'd give my favorite nephew a lift into town, since I had to come out here anyway," he answered, giving some feeble tale about a ticket mixup.

Robbie didn't seem to notice. "My good luck. Guess it's still with me." Robbie shouldered his bag and swung into step with Mark.

"Lucky? I take it you won the debate," Mark said, hoping it was that success, and not the anticipation of seeing Miss Divine, that put the sparkle in the boy's eyes.

"Yep. You're looking at the champ of the champion team, old man."

"Well, well. Congratulations."

Robbie was enthusiastic as they made their way to the parking lot and gave a detailed report on the pros and cons and the way his team had whipped all the rest.

"Okay, so I believe you," said Mark. "Guess you've inherited my way with words."

"Inherited more than that," Robbie said, grinning. "Picked up some of that old marksmanship with the womenfolk, too, old man."

"Oh?" Here it comes, thought Mark. Now he'll tell me about the delicious Deedee Divine.

"Yep." Robbie swung his bag into the trunk Mark had opened. "There was this most delectable blonde on the Yale team, you see. All the guys were after her. But I took a note from your technique, Mark. I played it cool." He laughed as he slid into the passenger seat. "It worked. Soon had her chasing me. Think I've talked her into joining me in Florida for the spring break."

"I see," said Mark, who didn't see at all. "What about Deedee Divine?" he almost asked, before he remembered he wasn't supposed to know anything about her. "Spring break, huh?" Maybe Robbie was turning into a playboy. Jasper had held him too tight, too long.

"Yep. Might even get her to transfer to Berkeley."

"I see," Mark said again, wondering at Robbie's enthusiasm for the blonde, and no mention of Deedee. "Er, how about, well, that, I take it, won't interfere with any other, er, connections?"

"Heck, no. And that's another way my luck held out. I had a thing going with this little dancer at Spike's Bar. That is, I thought I had something going...thought she felt the same way, you know. And then, just before I left, she turned me down flat! I was really mad."

"Turned you down? Before you left?" Mark's mind reeled as he tried to absorb this fact.

"Yeah. Bombed me out. We'd been having this grand time, you see. And there I was presenting her with this big diamond engagement ring. And she comes on sounding like Gramps—I'm too young to know my own mind, give myself time to explore, lots of other women out there and all that rubbish. Man! Like I say, I was mad. But you know something, Mark? Damn if she wasn't right. I'd sure hate to be all tied up when Debbie... That's the blonde from Yale. Do you think I'd be pushing it if I sent her a diamond bracelet, Mark?"

Mark wasn't listening. She had turned Robbie down. Before he left. There wasn't going to be any marriage that he had shelled out four hundred thousand dollars to prevent!

Damn! He meant to have another talk with Miss Deedee Divine!

CHAPTER THREE

MARK dropped Robbie at his frat house and drove off in a blind fury.

That lying, conniving little bitch had conned him out of four hundred thousand dollars! Not him. Jasper. So he couldn't stop payment. Too late anyway. How long was it? Six days. Hell, she would have cashed it first thing. Jasper could confirm, but he'd rather not let the old man know he'd been had! A patsy!

He screeched to a stop at a red light and pounded his fist on the steering wheel. To think he'd been taken in by a sweet-looking, fast-thinking, clever talking, deceitful, Academy-award-winning, gold-digging bitch! Well, it's not over yet, Miss Deedee double-dealing Divine! We're going to have it out if I have to sit at Spike's all night.

Not that she'd be there. Probably sunning herself at some fancy resort like the French Riviera or cruising on the Caribbean, living it up with all that loot.

Wherever you are, I'll find you, he vowed. Spike's was the place to start.

Thank goodness this was her last night, Terri thought as she donned her harem costume. The long nights after a long day at the office were

beginning to tell on her. Coupled with moving
from one apartment to another and worrying
about Mom. Please, please, let her be all right,
Terri prayed as she slipped the sils on her fingers.
For some reason, tonight she felt an almost over-
whelming sense of despair. Maybe she counted
too much on the bone marrow transplant. This
process, the doctor had said, was still in the experimental stage, and some people didn't
respond.

Oh, what kind of thinking was this! Never
harbor a negative thought. She forced a smile as
she fastened her jeweled belt. Everything was
going so well. Mom and Aunt Meg had passed
all the tests and the transplant would take place
tomorrow. This was her last night at Spike's, so
she could fly up to visit her mother on the
weekend. She shut her eyes, pictured herself
talking to the doctor, hearing him say, "A
tremendous success, no complications. Indications are that your mother will have a full
recovery."

She kept the happy thought, wore the bright
smile and went into her dance.

She finished her act, changed into the white
dress and returned for her social drinking duties.
Came face to face with Mark Denton.

"Still here, I see. How fortunate," he said
through clenched teeth. "I think we have some
unfinished business to discuss."

"Oh?" She swallowed, but couldn't drown the
panic. "No. That is, we..." She didn't know what
she meant to say, but he gave her no chance. He

clamped a firm hand on her elbow, propelled her
to the secluded booth and almost slammed her
into a seat.

"Took me in, didn't you!" He kept his voice
low, but he looked like a thundercloud about to
burst.

He knew! Robbie had told him and he had
come to take back the money. He couldn't. She
had already paid most of it out for the surgery,
so he couldn't get it. Still, she was glad he didn't
know where it was.

"Fed me a pack of lies, didn't you?"

She shook her head, not quite able to find her
voice.

"Oh, yes, you did. And don't give me that
innocent baby-face facade! I know what's behind
it. A lying, cheating, double-dealing— Go
away!" Terri jumped, but it was to Vashti he
spoke. "And take that damn thing with you,"
he added, sending the champagne bucket
spinning across the table.

Vashti grabbed it just in time to keep it from
toppling over, glanced at Terri and scurried away.
That quick glance, that scared-rabbit retreat,
summoned Terri's courage. She would not be in-
timidated by this society bully with his know-it-
all holier-than-thou arrogance! She had not
sought him. He had come to her. She had not
asked him for anything. He had offered. She
found her voice.

"You are mistaken. I told no lie."

"Oh? How about all those tearful prot-estations? All that stuff about what was between you and Robbie?"

"You assumed what was between us. I never said—"

"No? What about all those goose bumps and chemistry and not fighting mother nature?"

"You said yourself that was no indication of deep affection." She almost giggled. He had said it. She had just gone along with him.

"Miss Divine, we're not playing a game. You conned me out of a vast sum of money. There are laws against con games. And legal resti-tution...like prison."

She gave a start. Could he send her to jail? She hadn't—

"I could be lenient, of course, might forget the whole incident. Should you return your ill-gotten gain."

"I can't return—" She stopped. Could he trace it, stop her payment to the doctor? She was being paranoid. Under a different name and to a Seattle doctor. Mom was safe. She would get the trans-plant tomorrow, and nothing was going to stop it. And she wasn't going to let this man bully her.

"Mr Denton, I did not con...did not ap-proach you, did not solicit one cent from you. You offered of your own free will to pay me." She swallowed. "For rendering a service."

"For breaking an engagement that didn't exist in the first place."

Terri drew herself up. "I think the payment was for a promise not to marry Robert Goodrich. I am honoring that promise."

"You didn't intend to marry him in the first place."

"That was not the point under consideration."

"The hell it wasn't!" He slammed a hand to the table. "You deliberately led me to believe that the marriage was all set."

"You are mistaken. It was you who brought up the subject of the proposed marriage, you who prattled about Robbie's youth and family opposition. You who insisted that wiser counsel should prevail."

"And you who set a price on that counsel."

"Wrong. You said the family had compassion, would compensate for my loss."

"Your loss! Chemistry and goose bumps!"

She shrugged. "Whatever. You offered compensation."

"I offered one hundred thousand dollars, fool that I was."

"Still, it was you who offered. I didn't—"

"Didn't go into an award-winning performance? All that stuff about whatever was between you and Robbie not being for sale."

"Well, it wasn't!"

"No, indeed!" he snorted. "Not until you had raised the stakes to half a million."

"Four hundred thousand."

"For nothing!"

"For my promise not to marry—"

"You weren't going to marry him anyway."

"Which had nothing to do with our agreement. I promised. You paid. I'm keeping my promise. And I'm keeping the compensation."

"Look, lady—and I use that term loosely—if you think we're going to let you get away with a half million dollars on a scam, anchored in half truths and innuendoes, you're mistaken!" He stood up, bent over the table and looked her straight in the eye. "Unless you return the whole or a substantial amount, we'll see you in court. And damn soon!"

Terri sat motionless as he stalked away. She was terrified. His last words, spoken in a hoarse whisper, were no idle threat. Would he have her arrested? Could he?

"So what's with the hotshot?" Vashti, balancing a loaded tray, jerked her head toward the departed man. "Got a gripe on, huh?"

Terri, still in a daze, nodded.

"Man, I thought he was going to bust me one." Vashti gave her a keen look. "You all right, kid?"

"Sure. I'm okay...fine." She had committed no crime. She had only...

"That's the stuff, kid. Don't let no jerk get you down. We get all kinds of bimbos in this joint." She touched Terri on the shoulder. "Better get going. Almost time for your number."

Terri stood, but her legs seemed heavy. Loaded with guilt. He was right.

A scam! Anchored on half truths and innuendoes. She had lied, cheated, wormed him out of four hundred thousand dollars.

But she was going to pay it back. She would start as soon as . . .

Stop kidding yourself! Four hundred thousand dollars? Never in a lifetime!

Could she get the money back? Stop the operation?

No. She wouldn't, even if she could. Mom was going to have her chance. She was glad she had gotten the money, no matter how.

No matter what the consequences.

Terri donned her costume and went out to dance.

"Now, let me get this straight." Nate Collins, the astute lawyer who had been his close friend since prep school, pulled his horn-rimmed glasses down on his nose and looked over them at Mark. "I am to take four hundred thousand dollars from your account and send same to Jasper Goodrich, indicating that said sum has been extracted from a Miss Deedee Divine who obtained same under fraudulent claims."

Mark waved his hand in a vague gesture. "Something like that. You know how to handle it." Jasper might be a fool with his money, but it wasn't fair that he should be parted from it when it was Mark who had been cheated. He'd explain to his uncle that he had learned Robbie was not as entangled as they had presumed and he had forced her to return the money.

"Um," said Nate. "And will this fund be, er, extracted from the said Miss Divine?"

"Damn right." In one way or another. But without the publicity that would expose Jasper's shenanigans—and not expose himself as a damn fool! "It must be handled discreetly," he said.

"I see. And just how is this sum to be discreetly extracted?"

"That's your job. You're the lawyer. Figure it out."

Nate glowered in exasperation. "It beats me how supposedly sensible people can get into the dumbest jams and expect me to pull them out!"

Mark chuckled. "Keeps your pockets padded, doesn't it?"

"A living, anyway, for me and a lot of other people. Might be cheaper to let her keep the dough."

"Rather your pockets than hers!"

"No joke, Mark. This kind of deal is complicated, and if pursued, could drag on and on." He sighed. "Now let's see. You made a contract with this woman."

"Contract?"

"A written agreement, spelling out the exact terms."

"No. No. Nothing written. We just—"

"A verbal agreement, I take it, relative to certain considerations."

"Damn right. She agreed not to marry Robbie and I shelled out four hundred thousand dollars." He stopped, jolted by the significant quirk of Nate's brows. More than being a fool, he hated looking like one. "The check. It was written. That proves something, doesn't it?" he stuttered.

"Oh, cool it, Mark. A verbal contract can be legally binding. And if this was some kind of scam, a con game..." He reached for one of his heavy law books. "There is a precedent where a con man was thrown into jail for—"

"No. Wait!" Mark said quickly, daunted by the thought of that innocent-looking girl with the teasing blue eyes being thrust into a cell among all kinds of vagrants. Damn it! He was doing it again. But he didn't want to go that far. "Well, hell," he said. "What good would her being in jail do me? I want my money back! Tell her if she doesn't return it we'll...we'll expose her!"

Nate grinned. "Like throwing the rabbit in the briar patch! It has been my experience that women of that, er, caliber welcome publicity, scandalous or otherwise. Serves to, er, boost their career."

Mark stared at him, feeling extremely frustrated. "I see what you mean. And damned if I want any publicity. Come to think of it, that's another part of the agreement, to keep her mouth shut. Uncle Jasper specifically requested that the whole thing be kept quiet."

"I see." Nate took off his glasses. "You don't want her thrown in jail. No publicity. This leaves us in a bit of a quandary." His lips twitched. "Sure you wouldn't just as soon let her keep the money?"

CHAPTER FOUR

THE man in the loud checkered jacket approached her as soon as she came into Spike's Tuesday night. "You're Ms Deedee Divine?"

"Yes." Terri nodded. Not the first man who wanted to engage her dance act for a special event or long-term. "But I'm not accepting any more engagements at the present time."

That seemed to amuse him. "You'll accept this one," he said, thrusting an envelope into her hand.

She watched the door slam behind him, then glanced at the envelope in her hand. It bore the letterhead of a lawyer. She felt a chill of apprehension, but resolutely slit it open.

A threat that she would be sued and hauled into court if she did not, within thirty days, reimburse said claimant of the sum extracted from him by fraudulent means. Legal jargon punctuated by herewiths and theretofors, culminating in the fact that she had, through verbal contract, accepted sum of four hundred thousand dollars in consideration of which her engagement to Robert Goodrich would be terminated. Since no such engagement did, in fact, exist, there was no consideration, which renders contract null and void. She was hereby ordered to return sum advanced to her to plaintiff forthwith. Failure to comply within thirty days would result in her being sued for fraud. The letter was signed by Nate Collins.

Feelings of anger, guilt and dismay flooded through her.

Anger. It was all Mark Denton's fault. She had not asked him for a darn thing. She had been going along, minding her own business, trying to figure out how to solve her own problems. Then he barged in, practically accusing her of seducing his precious nephew, and prattling on about not being fair to herself or to Robbie, and offering to compensate for her loss. That's right. He was the one who mentioned compensation. She had never given a thought nor asked—

But you snatched it, didn't you? As soon as you caught on to what was what?

What was I supposed to do with him dangling all that loot right in front of me when I needed it for Mom? I'm glad I did it and I'd do it again. So there!

Dismay. Oh, God, what's going to happen now? Fraud. They could put you in jail for that, couldn't they? I can't go to jail. There's my job. And Mom.

She looked again at the letter. It was addressed to Ms Deedee Divine at Spike's Bar. He didn't know who she was or where she lived. If she hadn't come back tonight to get Mom's good luck charm from Vashti... "I must have lost it when I fainted that night," Delia, still in recovery and still a little dazed, had complained. "Ask Vashti."

Vashti had confirmed that she had it, and Terri had come tonight to get it. If she hadn't she would never have received the summons. Darn!

She hadn't told anybody where she was moving and she had left no forwarding address on account of Robbie, but... Oh, yes, the law could track you down.

Maybe she ought to hire a lawyer.

She couldn't afford a lawyer.

Well, darn it, Terri Thompson, use your brain! Dig up some of that business law you crammed into your head.

There could be all kinds of misconceptions in a verbal contract, couldn't there? And she had not willfully deceived or tried to con him or anything. She had just... Oh, heck, she had always meant to pay it back, hadn't she? Maybe if she started to repay it. She thought. She had reserved fifty thousand for Mom's hospital expense and the stay in Seattle. But it might not take all of that. If she returned twenty thousand... She went to the condo and drafted a letter.

Nate's face was expressionless as he studied his friend. "Well?"

Mark looked at him, then at the letter, reading it more carefully this time.

My dear Mr Collins,
Pursuant to your letter of May 4, instituting fraudulent claims against me on behalf of your client, Mark Denton, it is imperative that the following facts be made clear.

There seems to be some misconception regarding the verbal contract between me and Mr Denton. It was my understanding that in return for his payment of four hundred thousand dollars, I promised not to marry Robert Goodrich, prior commitment or noncommitment notwithstanding. I am honoring that promise. His claim that a fixed engagement was necessary consideration for such a promise comes as a total surprise to me.

"That's a damn lie!" Mark exclaimed to the expressionless Nate. "You should have heard that spiel about chemistry and goose bumps and their relationship not being for sale!"

Nate's lips twitched, barely suppressing a smile.

"Strikes you as funny, huh? Damn!" he muttered as he returned to the letter.

However, I realize that verbal contracts can be misconstrued and Mr Denton might have been confused about the terms. His conception of the issues involved clearly differs from mine. I do not wish to take advantage of this misconception, nor defraud him of funds for which he feels he has received no consideration. Therefore, I hereby agree to reimburse to him the amount of four hundred thousand dollars.

However, you do understand that some time has elapsed since I received the money, and prior commitments make it impossible for me to pay the entire amount at this time. I am hereby enclosing a check in the amount of twenty thousand dollars along with a signed note to the effect that a monthly sum of one hundred dollars will be sent to claimant until the entire amount, with interest, has been paid.

I hope you will accept the above as an expression of good faith. Thanking you in advance, I am,

Very truly yours,
Deedee Divine

"Impossible!"

Nate's eyebrows lifted.

"She couldn't have spent three hundred and eighty thousand dollars in ten days, could she?"

Nate shrugged. "That's beside the point."

"But that is the point."

"No. The point is that you're dealing with a very smart cookie or one who's getting expert legal advice from somewhere."

"Oh?"

"She's right. Verbal contracts, by their very nature, are—" again the raised eyebrows "—shall we say, rather vague, and can often, purposefully or otherwise, be misconstrued. The twenty thousand is a healthy indication of her good intention as well as good faith."

"This—" he thrust the check onto the desk "—is a mere fraction of what she owes me."

"Best take it and run. It'll be a cold day in hell before you get another cent."

"Oh, no! We've still got her promissory note."

"Notes can be defaulted. We can't put people into prison for debt, as we can for fraud. In other words, Mark, she's off the hook."

"Not if we don't accept the check. If we hauled her into court—"

"We'd lose. And you might relish looking like a fool but I don't."

"The devil we'd lose. She deliberately conned me, and—" He was halted by Nate's derisive snort.

"Who, in his right mind, would believe that the widely read columnist, Mark Denton, who so astutely analyzes current events, could be hoodwinked into shelling out such a monstrous sum without solid grounds for doing so?"

"I see what you mean."

"And speaking of publicity, your colleagues would have a ball." Mark cringed. "I'm afraïd, old buddy, she has you over a barrel."

Mark stared at his friend, lost in thought.

It wasn't the money. It was the disappointment. She hadn't looked like the kind of woman who would hoodwink a guy. She had such a dignity of bearing, such an innocent look.

Damn! The conniving little bitch had not only cheated, but had outwitted him, and there was nothing he could do about it! He felt like a tiger in a cage, grinding his teeth and shaking the bars, helpless. Never mind that it didn't make the papers. In his mind's eye, she stood outside the cage laughing and laughing.

Well, damn it, she wasn't going to get away with it!

She had sent a cashier's check with no return address. Spike's was his only lead.

She wasn't there. Replaced by Bootsie Lee, a topless dancer, with too much figure and very little grace.

"These dancers come and go," Spike said. "I never bother with an address."

"Never did know where she lived," the waitress declared. "Anyway, she said she was moving from wherever it was."

That figures, Mark thought. And maybe it's a good thing. If I wring her bloody neck, I'd land in jail!

"Taken flight!" he reported to Nate. "Probably on the Concorde with all that money I'll never see again."

"Cool it," Nate advised. "Not enough to bust a blood vessel over."

Neither realized that the rage choking Mark Denton had nothing to do with money. It was the disappearance of a pair of teasing blue eyes.

Mom was progressing nicely. No complications, the doctor had said. One more week and she could move to the little apartment Terri and Aunt Meg had rented near the hospital.

So Terri returned to San Francisco early Sunday in a jubilant mood. I'm glad I decided to share this condo with Angie, she thought, though the rent is steeper than I would have wished. That was because of the added expense of the furnishings, also leased from Marge. But the beautifully upholstered furniture and exquisite accessories in muted tones of lavender matched perfectly with the plush wall to wall carpet, and gave that final touch of elegance. Angie was not at home, but the afternoon sun pouring through the wide windows was a warm, cheerful greeting. And it will be just as cheerful, she thought, when the rain pounds against the windows and we light a fire in the stone fireplace. Mom will love it.

One thing clouded her mind. Her check had not been cashed, and no letter awaited her at Spike's Place, the only address they would have. Had they or had they not accepted her offer? She thought of calling the attorney's office, but decided against it. Best to just disappear if they were of a mind to haul her into court.

Anyway, they hadn't returned her check, and if she kept her part of the bargain, which she meant to do, that would show good faith, wouldn't it? All she had to do was pay the stuffed shirt one hundred dollars a month for the rest of her life! And why, for goodness sake, was she mad at him? She should be grateful and glad to pay back the money that had sent Mom on the road to recovery. Now, with Mom on the mend, she was free to concentrate on her work.

Not quite free. The apprehension remained. Was she off the hook or not?

During the following weeks, Terri managed to push the episode from her mind and immerse herself in her job. At the California State Commission on Economic Development, her responsibility was to assess applications for small business loans and make recommendations for authorization for allotment of funds to applicants. She loved what she was doing and the people she met. Like Eliza Carr. "Making these stuffed animals was just a hobby, you know. Then my husband died... Now it's the only income for me and the kids. If I could convert the basement and get enough money to send out catalogues..."

"Or like Joe Daniels," she told Angie on one of the rare occasions when they were both home and making dinner together. "That young man who was in the office today. He's not only a dream of a dancer but he has the special knack of imparting his talent to others. I've seen some of his groups perform. And he's just teaching part time at the most unsuitable places. Terrible floors and no bars or mirrors. If he had his own place..."

"Which you'll be sure he gets," Angie said, grinning. "Do you know your trouble, Terri?"

"I know yours. You're burning the potatoes again," Terri said, snatching the pot from the stove. "Got it just in time. Hand me a bowl."

Angie handed her the bowl, but was not diverted. "Thing is, I think you're in the wrong occupation. I'm going to read your horoscope."

"Oh, no, please." Terri groaned. Angie was a delightful and compatible roommate, but Terri had had it with the psychic phenomena. "You've already done numerology and—" She stopped, aware that her friend was not listening.

Angie's face had taken on that speculative out-of-this-world stare. "Too soft. More into people than business."

"Oh, Angie!"

"It's true, Terri. You were more concerned that the Carr woman could work at home and be with her children than whether her little business would stimulate the economy. And take this Joe Daniels."

"A dance studio is good business," Terri said.

"Maybe."

"He's going to hire teachers, give performances. He's even making televised demonstrations that will be distributed through major stores, certainly a boost to the economy."

But Angie was dubious and the argument continued while they made salad and broiled the chops. As they ate, Angie still did not let up. "You really ought to join LLL," she told Terri.

"Huh?"

"That group I meet with every second Tuesday, Life, Love, Living."

"Oh."

"You get to delve into your real self and make the most out of life. For instance, once you realize the difference between selfish and selfless you understand the true meaning of 'First of all to thine own self be true'."

"I see."

"You, Terri, are clearly a selfless person. Too busy seeing to other people's happiness to make yourself happy."

"I am happy."

"When all you do is work and run up to Seattle to see about your mom? Since when have you been out on a date?"

Terri was about to say that dating was not always a measure of true happiness when the phone rang and Angie dashed to answer. From Angie's comments, she guessed that it was Sid Farmer, an affluent fellow tenant, whose acquaintance Angie had managed through vigilant visualization and frequent trips to the exercise room.

Angie returned to the table, beaming. "Guess what? Sid's a member of the yacht club."

"Oh?"

"Just as I visualized. I keep telling you it works. And he's invited me to a dance there tomorrow evening."

"That's nice, Angie."

"And I asked if you could go along with us and he said of course. Maybe you ought to wear—"

"Wait a minute. Won't I be a bit of a fifth wheel?"

"Well, yes, to tell the truth, you will." Angie gave a sigh.

"So why are you burdening yourself and poor Sid who, I am sure would rather have you alone?"

"The thing is, I'm trying to achieve balance, you see."

"Balance?"

"I tend to lean toward selfish. The counselor at LLL suggests that if I train myself to do more selfless things, like getting you out of the doldrums—''

Terri burst out laughing. ''Angie, you're too much. I'm not in the doldrums.'' But when she saw that Angie was quite serious, and would rather take her than someone else who might be after Sid, she accepted the invitation. Why not? She loved to dance and she'd like to have a look inside that exclusive club.

The yacht club was all that it promised to be with its several exquisitely furnished anterooms, all carrying out the decorative theme featuring sail-boats and sailing appurtenances. The dance was held in the main dining room. Dining tables had been arranged in a semicircle to accommodate a wide area for dancing. It was a gala affair, and she was glad she had come. Sid was an affable host, lavish with introductions, and she did not lack for partners. She danced and danced, easily attuned to the haunting old melodies or rollicking new ones rendered by the combo in Latin attire. Now everyone was taking a breather while the combo took a break. Another couple had joined their table, and Terri listened contentedly to the lively chatter of the others. She glanced idly around the room, noting how impressively the subdued lights reflected upon the beads and colorful cocktail dresses of the well-groomed women and the correct black and white tuxedos of their escorts. Then she saw him. He was seated at a table only a few feet away and he was staring directly at her.

Quickly she averted her eyes. He didn't recognize her. He couldn't. Could he?

Terri smiled at the brunette beside her who was talking about the value of exercise. "Do you do aerobics?" she asked Terri.

"Yes . . . oh, no." She hated aerobics. All that jerking. A quick glance. He was still watching her.

"You ought to try it. It really keeps you fit."

"I might do that." Sit still. No reason to panic. In this setting and without her wig, he'd never recognize her.

It was her. He was sure of it. She had cut that long black hair and dyed it. But even with the auburn curls that framed it, he could never have mistaken that heart-shaped face, that slightly tilted little nose. That was Miss Deedee Divine from Spike's Bar, and what the devil was she doing here?

Well, he meant to find out. How fortunate that he had decided on the spur of the moment to drop in at the club tonight.

He had gotten up and was walking toward their table. What was she to do? Nothing. He didn't know who she was. And even if he did . . . He hadn't cashed the check, but he hadn't returned it, either. Didn't that mean he had accepted her plan? Why was she so jittery?

"The Elite Aerobics Center? Oh, yes, that's not too far from our condo," she said to the brunette. "I'll look in there."

The brunette had stopped listening. She was smiling at Mark Denton. "Mark! So you decided to favor us. Are you alone?'' At his nod, she said, "Pull up a chair and join us. Move over, Bob," she said to her husband as she slid her chair over, making room for Denton between herself and Terri.

Terri swallowed, gasped and tried to look composed as Mark seated himself right next to her. He didn't seem to take special notice of her, thank goodness. He was greeting the others at the table, all of whom seemed to know him, except Angie, of course. That was quickly remedied as Sid introduced them. "Angie Parker and Terri Thompson, Mark. And this gentleman, ladies, is the famous columnist Mark Denton, whose mug and wit you might have scanned in your daily *Chronicle*. That is, if that kind of pervasive intellectualism appeals to you."

"Thanks a lot, old buddy." He was laughing with his friends and had acknowledged the introduction with a casual nod. Some of the fear subsided. He didn't recognize her!

Mark was finding it hard to keep his cool. Terri Thompson, my foot! Deedee Divine. No way could she hide those teasing blue eyes or that tiny dimple that lurked in the corner of her mouth. Did she take him for a complete fool? And what kind of scam was she up to?

"Miss . . . Thompson, did you say?" he asked, turning to her.

"Yes."

"New in the city?"

"No. Well, that is, yes. I've only lived here for about three months."

"Oh? And what brings you to our fair city?"

"My job." And stop asking all those stupid questions and inspecting me with that steely, penetrating stare. If you know who I am, say so and be done with it!

"Ah, music. Shall we dance, Miss... No, we mustn't be so formal. Terri?"

She took the hand held out to her and allowed him to lead her to the dance floor. The combo was playing a slow seductive accompaniment to the soloist whose throaty voice belted out the words of an old love song. His arm went around her, pulling her close, and he smiled at her in a way that sent a thrill spinning through her whole being. A thrill that had nothing to do with the fear of being recognized.

CHAPTER FIVE

THIS was crazy.

She said she was Terri Thompson. He knew for a fact that she was Deedee Divine. It didn't seem to matter. The face reflected in the dim light was very pale, the eyes downcast, hidden from him. He looked at the long lashes brushing her cheeks, breathed in the sweet spicy fragrance drifting from the chestnut curls that barely reached his shoulder and felt a strange urge to keep her forever in the shelter of his arms. He moved as if in a dream to the strains of a distant seductive melody that drummed softly in his ears.

The music stopped, jolting him out of the euphoria. People jostled against him and there was a general hubbub of talk and laughter. Someone slapped him on the shoulder. "Mark. Didn't know you were back."

He turned to see one of the editors from the *Chronicle*. "Oh, hi. Yeah, just got back last night." During this brief exchange, he became aware that she was moving away. Quickly he reached for her. Fate had delivered the cheating little con artist into his hands, and this time he didn't mean to let her get away. Not sure what he meant to do with her, he simply took her hand for the next dance. As it turned out, for the next five, a series of Latin numbers.

Right down his alley. He had traveled extensively in Spain as well as Mexico, and had learned much from several exquisite and expert partners. But none that matched the grace and expertise of this one. As light as a feather on her feet, she followed with precise ease his execution of the rumba, the samba, and the cha-cha. He watched with fascination the rhythmic undulation of her shoulders, the graceful sway of her hips as she swirled away from or returned to his waiting arms. Never had he enjoyed dancing so much. He refused to relinquish her to any other partner.

"You are an excellent dancer," he said, during one interlude. "Are you, by chance, a professional?" If she could pretend they had never before laid eyes on each other, then so could he.

He caught the wary look quickly disguised by the shake of her head. "Oh, no."

An excellent liar, as well, he thought. But what he said was, "Then I think you've missed your calling. You're a natural."

"I might say the same for you," was her quick response. "Never have I danced with anyone so attuned to the music and so easy to follow."

"Flattery will get you anything," he said, chuckling. "Like a cool drink to quench your thirst. Come." He led her, not back to her table, but toward the bar at the other end of the room. He wanted to keep her to himself. Find out what her game was. Nate was probably right. It'd be a cold day in hell before he got his money back. But he had a hankering to find out just what she was doing with it.

"It's not flattery," she said earnestly. "I've never danced with any man who knew those Latin steps so well." She did not add, "except a professional," not wanting to hint of any such connection. It seemed he had not recognized her, but this kind of talk made her nervous. "I get the impression," she said, hastening to change the subject, "that you've just returned from a trip."

"Yes," he said. "I'm just back from Olympia."

She gasped, for the moment forgetting about herself... The news media was full of the civil strife in Olympia, the havoc, destruction and bloodshed. "How...how long were you there?" she asked, not quite sure why his being there bothered her.

"Only five days," he said as they settled on bar stools.

"Isn't it rather dangerous? I mean being right in the middle of it?" There had been reports of horrible incidents.

"A bit. But where there's news..." He shrugged.

She frowned. "I haven't seen anything in your column about Olympia."

"So you read me?" He smiled. First time she had seen that warm, winning smile. Now she was sure he didn't know her. That smile was not for the likes of a Miss Deedee Divine!

"Haven't quite thrashed it out in my mind yet," he said.

She studied him as he turned to the bartender who, like everyone else in the club, seemed to know him. He was so relaxed, as if he didn't have a care in the world. He had danced so jubilantly with her, and was now casually exchanging quips with the barman. Hard to imagine that yesterday he had been dodging bullets in Olympia. Observing. Thinking about it before—

"You always do that, don't you?" she said, as he handed her a drink.

"Do what?"

"Analyze a situation carefully before you write about it." And maybe that's why his writing was always so clear and concise, she thought, taking a sip of the drink. More potent than she would have liked, but delicious and refreshing. "Thank you. I like it," she said.

"Good. Mixed especially for you." There was that smile again. She was drowning in it. Quickly she averted her eyes. "So," she said brightly. "When are we to get your assessment of the crisis in Olympia?"

"I don't know." He sighed. "It's hard to make sense of a senseless situation."

"It is senseless, isn't it? What is it really all about?"

"History." He twirled the ice in his glass, as if suddenly angry. "Wounds never healed. Feuds never buried. Retribution for wrongs a hundred years old."

"Yes. Oh, yes. I see what you mean." She saw more. His heart was in it, whatever he wrote. She thought of Olympia and shared his dismay. "So stupid," she said. "To hold grudges . . . and for so long."

"So, in your opinion, forgiveness is the simple answer?"

"Of course."

"Not always easy to forget and forgive."

"True. What is that expression? Oh, yes... to err is human, to forgive divine."

His head jerked up. Why was he looking at her like that?

"That's your answer, is it? To any dirty, double-dealing trick somebody plays on you? Just forget and forgive?"

Whatever had she said to set him off? And weren't they still talking about Olympia? Or... Her blood ran cold.

He was glaring at her. "Even if there's no repentance? No atonement?"

Darn it, she was atoning! Wasn't she paying him back? Stop it, she cautioned herself. He can't know you. "Don't be ridiculous!" she said, steadily sticking to Olympia. "Who's around to atone for a hundred-year-old crime? And certainly, in this case, forgiveness would prevent a lot of bloodshed."

He grinned and gave a little nod as if in salute. "You're right, of course. Is that the policy I should adopt in my analysis?"

"I wouldn't dream of trying to advise Mark Denton," she said, taking a deep breath as relief flooded through her. "But it would make sense."

"Right. I think you've solved my problem, Miss Thompson. Could I possibly persuade you to join my staff?"

"You have a staff?" she asked, surprised.

"Certainly I have a staff. Did you think—?"

"Guess I didn't think," she said, feeling an impulse to giggle. "I pictured you off all by your lonesome, frowning at your notes, plugging away at a typewriter. Or behind some barricade, making notes while bullets whined around you. Or hidden in a basement while some sneak pours political secrets into your ear. Or—"

"Okay. Okay. Stop!" he said, bursting into a hearty laugh. "What kind of novels have you been reading? When I tell you that I work in an ordinary office with the able assistance of a secretary, researcher and leg man surrounded by telephones, computers and fax machines, does my charisma rating drop?"

"Several points," she said, making a face. "And I won't work for you. No fun."

"I was afraid of that. So let's dance while we can. I've been expecting interference any minute," he said, glancing rather anxiously at her table.

"No danger of that. I'm a fifth wheel."

"Oh?"

"I came with my roommate and her date. She's trying to achieve balance."

"Balance?"

"Never mind," she said, chuckling at his puzzled look. "I'm sure they're glad to dump me."

"Oh, in that case, join this one wheeler and make a delightful twosome." She watched the smile start at the corner of his mouth, spread across his face and settle in his eyes. How could a man with such laughing blue eyes be a one wheeler? He was handsome, interesting to talk to and an excellent dancer. So how, she wondered, in this room full of beautiful women, had she managed to keep him all to herself for one whole hour? It seemed like minutes but it must have been that long, or longer, she thought, as he led her to the dance floor.

However, as the evening progressed, she realized that it was he, not she, cleverly isolating them from would-be intruders. He could be engaged in a cheerful conversation one minute, and in the next give a dismissive nod, disengaging himself to turn to her. She felt a strange exultation. He liked her, enjoyed being with her, preferred her company above that of any of the exquisitely gowned women. She gloated in the knowledge and exerted herself to be charming. Until she became lost in pure bliss, forgetting to be anything but happy. Dancing the night away, talking and joking, lost to everything but the laughter in a pair of dark blue eyes.

When he suggested a breath of fresh air, she followed in a trancelike state to the deck of the clubhouse. Enchantment. The night was warm. No breeze stirred and a full golden moon hung over the bay. Terri, blissfully unaware of the murmur of voices, the groups of other couples seated or strolling about, leaned against the balustrade and looked down at the sailing crafts that lined the wharf.

"That must be fun," she said.

"What?" he asked, looking at her.

"Sailing." On any of them, she thought. To traverse the ocean on one of those luxurious yachts. Or just to skim across the bay in one of the sailboats.

"You'd like that?"

"Oh, yes."

"Then I'll take you," he said. "When would you—?"

Quickly she turned to him. "You have a boat? One of those?"

He nodded.

Yes, she thought, remembering that he must be rich. Probably owned one of those big yachts like that one with lights twinkling from the portholes.

"Not a very big one. That forty-foot motor cruiser," he said, pointing. "Between that yacht and that small sailing skiff. Can you see it?" The sleek outlines of the white cruiser were dimly reflected in the lights from the yacht, and she nodded. "Would you like to go sailing with me?"

"Oh, yes. I'd love it." Alone with him, sailing across the water. She stared at him, thinking how it would be.

"Then we'll set a date, shall we?" She nodded. "And seal it like this?" He bent and touched his lips to hers.

Such a light touch. But it was like a bolt of lightning, spiraling through her and settling, as if permanently, in her pounding heart. Jolting her into reality. Alerting her to danger. The danger of falling in love with a man who would hate her if he knew...

She had no thought but to escape.

"Yes. Indeed we must. Go sailing, I mean," she said, her hurried words as befuddled as her jumbled emotions. "Soon. But not too soon. So busy. My job. No time for dating...sailing. And my goodness, it's late. Angie will be wondering. I must find her."

"Wait." He clasped her hand. "Hadn't we better set—?"

"Some other time. Lovely evening. Thanks. Goodbye." She broke loose and sped away before he could stop her. He was about to follow. She was glad to hear someone call, "Just a minute, Mark. I've been wanting to ask you..."

When he reached the ballroom, she was nowhere to be seen. Damn! If that publisher hadn't stopped him...

He looked around for Sid. That must have been who she was with. He introduced her. But Sid was not in the ballroom, either, nor was he in the lobby among those slowly departing. Damn!

She had cut out in a hurry. As if she suddenly remembered. Deedee Divine. He was sure of it now. As if he had had any doubt!

Just as well. That woman was dangerously bewitching. Uncanny the way she had of drawing you in, like a magnet, so that all sense of reality disappeared and she was all there was. The invitation in those teasing come-play-with-me eyes, that secretive smile on her lips curving in an enticing promise... Those lips. So sweetly yielding, even in that one brief moment.

Lord, yes! He was well out of it. He chuckled, remembering her advice—forgive and forget. Some nerve. She needn't think he meant to forgive the dirty deal she had pulled. But...oh, the hell with it! He sure meant to forget her.

Trouble was, he couldn't. Her essence pervaded his senses, wherever he was, whatever he was doing, boarding a plane, conducting an interview, writing about Olympia and the tragedy of unforgiveness.

Then he got a call from Nate. "It seems I was wrong, old buddy."

"Oh?"

"You might recoup if you stick around for fifty years."

"What are you talking about?"

"About the check I just received from Miss Deedee Divine. One hundred bucks. Right on time. As promised."

He was immensely pleased, ready to absolve her of any guilt. He would see her and... "Good. So she has surfaced. Where—?"

"Not exactly surfaced. Same deal as before. Cashier's check. No return address."

Still hiding in the flimsy disguise of Terri Thompson. Did she take him for a fool? Then why had she sent the check? Good faith. To fend him off in case he was suspicious and could put a spoke in whatever game she was playing.

Oh, forget her!

He might have, had he not paid a visit to his mother. He found her preparing to go out.

"To the opera. We made up a party for opening night. The Tollivers, the Websters and Dan Bell. I'm so glad you stopped by, Mark. I asked them all by for cocktails and you can be host. How fortunate that you dropped by."

"Sure I won't be usurping Dan?" he teased, as he kissed her. Helene Denton, a widow for five years, did not lack for male companions, and Dan was the most constant.

"Dan's always late. Now, go say hello to Mary and see how she's doing with the canapés. There are the Tollivers. I'll get the door."

Mark smiled. Having made him feel needed and having dispensed him to the kitchen to make Mary know she was more a friend than her housekeeper, his mother was now being equally gracious to her guests. He liked his mother.

After a convivial hour, the party was preparing to leave, and she sent him upstairs to fetch her opera glasses. "I think I left them on the bedside table."

Yes, they were there. And, beside them, the gift his father had given to his mother long before he was born. Carefully encased in a silver frame was the poem inscribed in old English script.

Wanted, a woman...
No saint understand,
But a womanly woman who, on every hand
Sheds the lustre of purity, goodness and grace,
Who carries her loveliness stamped on her face,
Whose wisdom's intuitive insight is deep,
Who's poised in her little world's centre,

and who
Is gentle, responsive, and tender and true,
Whose sweetness and graciousness fit like a
gown...
Do you think I might find such a one in this
town?

Yes. Dad had found her. Mom was that kind
of woman.

And why did another face swim before his eyes,
a face that haunted him and—

"Mark, did you find them?" his mother called.
"We mustn't be late. On that table, right by my
bed."

"Coming!" He picked up the glasses and ran
downstairs.

Now the poem began to haunt him as much as
the face. Especially the words, "no saint,
understand".

Terri Deedee Divine Thompson was surely no
saint.

But she was paying him back, wasn't she?
Maybe she really had misunderstood.

Misunderstood hell! She had deliberately
tricked him.

Her face. There was something so innocent and
straightforward... that is, when she wasn't being
conniving or defiant!

Maybe there was a good reason...

Oh, sure! Like setting herself up as some rich
society dame so she could hook another sucker.

One rainy Sunday afternoon he ran into Sid at
the club. He had finished his routine, showered

and was dressing when he spotted him. "At the club dance the other night. You were with two women."

Sid, puffing on the treadmill, looked blank for a moment, then reconnoitered. "Oh, yeah. Those two. Weird, man."

"Weird?"

"Spaced out." Sid got off the treadmill and began to lift weights.

"Oh." He tied his shoe and stood up straight, thinking. Drugs? Was she financing a habit?

Sid lifted, grunted and grinned. "Or maybe I should say out in space."

"Meaning?"

"Fathoming the secrets of the universe and the forces that control our destiny." Sid's chuckle hovered between mystery and mockery. "Angie's been trying to get me into one of those groupie setups."

"Oh. They live in a commune?"

"No. In a condo in my complex. That's why I'm exercising over here. That Angie is hard to avoid. Telling me what I could learn from the sessions on living and loving." Sid's chuckle rang out in hearty laughter. "Told her I could teach that myself!"

When he pressed the bell at the condo, the door was opened by the woman with the sleek pixie haircut.

"Hello!" she said, instant recognition in her penetrating dark eyes. "Come in. I've been expecting you."

"Oh?" He tried to mask his surprise. "Well, er, yes. I'm Mark Denton and I came to see—"

"I know. Terri. Have a seat. She'll be back in a moment. Would you like a cup of tea or something stronger perhaps?"

"No. Nothing, thank you." But he allowed her to take his raincoat and sat on the sofa, wondering why he had come and how she knew he was coming. "So. You were, er, expecting me?"

She nodded and sat, in Buddhalike fashion, where she had evidently been sitting among several carefully arranged cards. "Please excuse me. I want to finish this," she said, picking up one of the cards. "I have to work things out myself before I really understand it."

"I see."

"Are you familiar with the science of numerology?"

He shook his head.

"It's fascinating. An intuitive interpretation or analysis of any entity you wish to understand."

"I see," he said again, although he didn't. Out in space. And she looked so ordinary. Barefoot, cutoff jeans, faded T-shirt. She was engrossed, making pencil notations on the cards, and he hated to disturb her. But he wanted to know. "You said you were expecting me?"

She looked up at him and smiled. "Oh, yes. The way you looked at her the other night...I suspected right away." She nodded emphatically. "You have known each other in another life. You and Terri."

He stared at her. Oh, yes, we've met. In this life, lady! He felt strangely disturbed. What kind of game were they playing? "Terri...Miss Thompson? You said she'd be returning in a moment?"

"Oh, yes. She's just taking a short walk."

"Walking?" He glanced at the rain splattering against the window. "In this?"

"Oh, Terri never minds the rain. But I suspect you know that."

"I?"

"Oh, yes. I strongly feel that you are soul mates and know each other well."

"Soul mates?"

"But I can't tell until— Listen, would you like me to do your chart?"

"Chart?"

"Your astrological chart. You see—"

"No. No, thank you. In fact, I'd better go." Before I get in any deeper, he thought.

But, once outside, a light rain blowing against his face, he felt a stronger impulse. To find her. She must be walking in the nearby park.

CHAPTER SIX

Terri walked aimlessly, heedless of the rain. Disconsolate.

Aunt Meg's call had really thrown her. Mom had been doing so well. Now she was back in the hospital, and it didn't sound good.

Terri hadn't said anything to Angie, not wanting to put it into words. "Words are more powerful than thoughts," was another of Angie's credos. So all she had said was, "I'm going for a short walk," before she bolted, too steeped in misery to listen to Angie's upbeat, "Think and feel whatever you desire and you'll get it" game.

Her practical mind could only grapple with the reality—test inconclusive. More tests. Probing. If the cancer had spread... If another transplant was needed... No way could she dream up another three hundred and fifty thousand dollars!

Poor Mom. Hadn't she been through enough? Terri wanted to fly to Seattle, put her arms around her, suffer with her through the tests. But Aunt Meg said, "No. There's nothing you can do here. We'll just have to wait. I'll call you."

She walked on, her tears mingling with the rain.

It was when he rounded the bend nearest the yacht club that he saw her. A lone figure in the empty park, a few yards away, trudging along the gravel path toward him. When she came close, he saw that her head was bare, and she wore only a light jacket, no raincoat. She walked, hands in her pockets, head bent, so oblivious that she bumped straight into him and would have fallen had he not caught her.

"I'm sorry," The face staring at him was ashen, and the eyes held the stricken look of a child lost and in pain. He wanted to pick her up, hold her close and comfort her. At least he could take off his raincoat and wrap it around her. Too late for that.

"You're drenched," he said. "You'd better get out of this weather and into some dry clothes."

"No. No, I'm fine." She tried to pull away, and he realized he was still holding her.

"Come. I'll help you back to your place."

"No. Not yet. I just want to... to think."

"Better do your thinking inside." Something was troubling her, and he wasn't about to leave her to wander around alone. She seemed reluctant to return to her apartment. Anyway, his boat was nearer, and that's where he took her, never even questioning his instinctive urge to care for her.

As the heat in the cabin of the cruiser began to penetrate, Terri shivered, as if just realizing she was cold. She looked down at Mark Denton, who had stooped to remove her loafers. "Why are you here?" she wondered aloud.

"I'm often here. This is my boat," he said, setting her shoes aside and pulling her up. "And you're here to get out of those clothes and into a hot shower."

She protested. He insisted.

Oh, hell, she thought, I am really cold and in no mood for hanky-panky.

The bathroom was small, but adequate. The hot water warmed her skin, soothed her nerves and helped to clear her mind. She must have been in a daze. She had been walking in the park and had bumped into Mark Denton. Why was he there? And why had he brought her here?

When she got out of the shower, she found that her wet clothes had been removed. A terry cloth robe, presumably for her use, hung from a hook on the door. It was much too large, but she felt snug and strangely comforted in the depths of the heavy fabric, smelling faintly of some refreshing after-shave lotion.

She looks better already, he thought, as she emerged from the bathroom. There was a rosy glow to her skin, and her hair was curling into those big gold-tinted ringlets. Had she had a permanent, as well, when she cut that long straight black hair?

Or... Was he losing his mind? Could there really be identical look-alikes in this world? Was this wide-eyed innocent, almost smothered in his bathrobe, no relation at all to a belly dancer he had encountered in a sleazy bar? Somehow, right now, it did not seem to matter.

"Sit here. Let's get these on your feet," he said, holding up a pair of his own heavy cotton socks.

She sat, as if still in a daze, and dutifully extended one foot. He slipped on the oversize sock and reached for her other foot. "Hungry?" he asked. "I am." But the erotic yearning evoked by the softness of that small slender foot had nothing to do with food.

She nodded, acutely conscious of his thumb against her arch, gently caressing. She was reluctant when he drew it away and put on the sock. She watched him go over to a cupboard and take down a can of soup. He looked so different in that blue polo shirt and Levi's, both rather worn. Not the elegant tuxedo man who had danced with her at the club, nor the stuffed shirt in the prim business suit who had insulted and bullied her at Spike's. Just an ordinary guy whose tall presence made her feel, for some reason, strangely contented...safe.

Because it had been he who had presented her with the means to save her Mom's life?

Only maybe it hadn't saved her. Thoughts of her mother surfaced, and again she was almost overwhelmed by the anxiety and fear. She felt the contentment slipping away and fought to hold on. She brushed the fears aside. Mom was going to be all right.

"I'd take you for that promised sail," he said, busy stirring soup, cutting into a loaf of French bread. "But it's too rough out there now."

Rough. But comforting...the sound of rain drumming on the roof and splashing against the windows, while inside all was warm and dry.

She pulled the robe closer about her and looked around. The stove, sink, hidden cupboards and sofa bunk beds, upholstered in a bright lemon yellow fabric. The leather cushions of the corner booth where she sat were also lemon yellow. The booth encircled a round table of black chrome. Everything neat and uncluttered except for her clothes, drying on a chair by a wall heater. She did not know how or why it had come about, but she liked being here.

He set the prepared food on the table, slid into the booth facing her and lifted his wineglass. "Chow."

Needing no urging, she took several spoonfuls of the steaming soup, bit into the crunchy bread topped with melted cheese and looked gratefully at him. "It's delicious," she said. "I didn't realize I was so hungry."

"I know." He swallowed, nodded. "Didn't realize much of anything, did you?"

That was true. She looked at him, wondering. "What were you doing in the park?"

"Looking for you."

"But how did you know...?"

"Your friend at the condo said you were taking a walk. I waited for you to come back, and when you didn't, I...well, I thought I might join you."

She felt a momentary surge of pleasure. He had sought her out. He liked her. He wouldn't if he knew. She sighed, hardly realizing that she did so.

"Something bothering you?" he asked, his voice gentle, concerned.

She nodded, looked at her soup.

"Want to talk about it?"

"No! Oh, no!" She shook her head, fighting the impulse to confide. His concern was for Terri

Thompson, not Deedee Divine. She remembered the fury on his face—"If you think I'm going to let you get away with a half million dollar scam..." It was almost a half million. The enormity of what she had done overwhelmed and scared her. She had cut all connection with Spike's, but she had checked at the bank and knew her checks had not been cashed. She was not yet off the hook, and he might be still searching.

He was watching her closely. "Sometimes, when we have a problem, talking it over with someone helps. What about...what's her name? Your friend at the condo."

"Angie? Oh, well, yes..." She hesitated. Terri hoped Angie hadn't mentioned Mom, though she was not quite sure how that might bring him closer to Deedee Divine. Thank goodness, Angie knew nothing of the belly dancing. Fearful of jeopardizing her position, Terri had not told anyone at the office about her stint at Spike's. Now she was doubly glad she hadn't. "Angie's great," she said. "But sometimes a bit way-out."

"I see." So maybe she's not as flaky as her friend. But very troubled about something, he thought, watching the play of emotions flit across her face. Such a sweet face. He wanted to take her in his arms, wipe the pain and anxiety from those eyes, kiss that quivering lip. "Tell me," he said, reaching across to gently cup her chin in his hand. "Perhaps I can help."

"No, you can't," she said, quickly drawing away. "There's nothing anyone can do. And, anyway, I'm quite all right now, thanks to you. Perhaps I should leave now,'' she added, starting to get up.

"Sit down and finish your soup before it gets cold," he said. "You can't leave until your clothes are dry."

"Yes. Forgot." She tried to smile as she sat back to finish her meal, but the scared look did not leave her eyes.

Wary of me. Why? Of course. He almost chuckled. She might not know that he knew who she was, but she knew damn well who he was. And if whatever troubled her had anything to do with the money she took from him...

Evidently she had no intention of coming clean. Well, he could play out this charade as long as she. Feeling a bit of irritation, he cleared the table and served coffee.

He couldn't hold onto his irritation. It was drowned in the surge of desire kindled by her close proximity and utter loveliness. She sat before him, loosely wrapped in his own robe, nothing beneath but the creamy soft sweetness of her skin, and she took his breath away. He couldn't take his eyes from the faintly throbbing pulse at her throat. He wanted to bury his face in her neck, kiss that throbbing pulse, slip his hands beneath the robe and... He sat up abruptly, transferring his gaze to her lips, her eyes, so lost, so vulnerable, so needful. Damn it! He couldn't seduce her, take advantage of the state she was in.

"How about a game of chess?" he said, his voice rather husky.

"What?" she asked, as if suddenly awakened from thoughts of her own.

"Chess." He got up and brought the game from a cabinet under one of the sofas.

"I...I don't know how to play," she said, as he, not looking at her, set the board on the table and began to lay out the pieces.

"Then you'd better learn. Nothing like it to take your mind from problems." And my mind from your body, he hoped, with some regret and not much conviction.

If the game did not help him, it did serve to divert Terri. She was a quick learner and an enthusiastic participant.

"Fascinating," she said, after he had explained the movement of the pieces and they had made a few plays. "How the king sits there in all his glory, never straying far from his station, while everyone else scurries all over the place, trying to protect him. Especially the queen," she added.

"Watch it! You're sounding like an avid feminist."

"Just stating the facts, sir," she said, giving him a bland look. "You will admit she travels farthest and works harder than any of the others."

"I don't know about that. Surely you are not discounting the dangerous hurdles made by the knights."

"Now that remark smacks of chauvinism," she said. "Like the king, who, I suspect, hardly appreciates his queen, you refuse to acknowledge the power of a woman."

"Depends upon the woman," he said, silently acknowledging that the woman before him had the power to make him forget everything but the pleasure of being with her. He found her quick wit and humor as intriguing as her beauty. He liked that little musical chuckle, and the way her eyes brimmed with laughter or sparkled with challenge. He was an expert player, she a complete novice, but he had never enjoyed a chess game so much in his life.

"I think," she said, some time later, "that my jeans are about as dry as they're going to get, and I'd better be on my way."

He realized with surprise that they had been sitting there almost three hours. Hours that seemed like minutes, and he still did not want to let her go.

She stood and bent toward him. "Thank you. You can have no idea how much this afternoon has meant to me. I was in such a funk." She hesitated, and he also stood, watching that troubled look again appear in her eyes. She gave a little laugh. "I don't know how it is, but I feel better now. As if...everything's going to be all right."

"I hope so," he said, taking her hands. "But, if not, if it doesn't turn out as you wish, tell me. Let me help you, whatever it is."

He means it, Terri thought. He really means it. Instinctively she moved toward him, and felt

his arms encircle and hold her close. It felt good
to be in his arms, to have the support of a lean,
muscular tower of strength. She snuggled into the
protective warmth, lifted her head, lips parted in
a grateful smile. Heard him gasp. Then his lips
were upon hers in a kiss that burned and spiraled
through her like a bolt of lightning, blotting out
all but passion, intense and longing. She wrapped
her arms around his neck and held on, never
wanting to let go. Waves of erotic pleasure surged
through her as his mouth traveled to the hollow
of her throat, teasing, enticing. One hand slipped
beneath the robe, gentle, caressing, arousing. She
gave a little moan.

Abruptly he drew back, took a deep breath and
reached out to draw the robe closer about her.

"You're right," he said, his voice a little husky.
"Time to go. I'll walk you home."

She had told him the truth. The hours spent with
him had made her feel better, as if her worry had
been all out of proportion. It was only natural
that they should bring Mom in for tests after
major experimental surgery. There would
probably be many more tests before she and Aunt
Meg left Seattle. And there was no need for her
to get into a tizzy each time.

She really slept very well that night. If visions
of a tall man with unruly black hair and a
crooked smile frequently appeared, they were
always pleasant visions as soothing as they were
exciting, lulling her into a happy, dreamlike state.
In one of those happy interludes between wake-

fulness and sleep, she thought of angels. Angie had a book about angels who appeared, in the most unlikely disguises, just when you needed them. He had come out of the blue with the money she needed for Mom, hadn't he? And tonight, when she had been walking around in a blue funk, hadn't he been there in spite of all that wind and rain? And he had brought her out of it and... No! That kiss, still vibrating and tingling within her, was not the kiss of an angel, but a man, virile, demanding, appealing. She had been sorry when he drew away.

Still, when he left her at her door, he had promised to keep in touch. She hoped he would.

Angel or not, he had lost all connection with the tyrant so threatening to Miss Deedee Divine.

Mark Denton had every intention of keeping in touch. When her arms had wound hungrily around his neck, those blue eyes alight with wanting, those delectable lips inviting, it had been hard not to take her then and there. She had been so sweet, so yielding, so... vulnerable. That was it. Vulnerable. No. That was not the time. When she came to him, and he vowed that she would, it would be with joy, not from despair.

He frowned as he got into his car and drove to his flat. What had troubled her so much that she had been oblivious to the rain and wind? She had been so reluctant that he had not pressed. But when they became closer... He smiled. They would become closer. He would see to that. Terri Thompson was the most captivating woman who had come his way in a long time. That night at the club... a dream of a dancer, an intelligent conversationalist, a delightful companion and tonight, when she managed to forget her problem, such a witty and cheerful adversary at chess. And... He would not think about that kiss. He would go home and take a cold shower.

He would, he promised himself, see more of Terri Thompson. Engaging as well as beautiful, with that mischievous teasing glint in those blue eyes, and that dimple that played at the corner of her mouth. If a certain conniving Deedee Divine possessed those eyes, that same dimple, it had, for the moment, completely escaped his mind.

CHAPTER SEVEN

TERRI tried to retain her good spirits, but she vacillated between hope and despair. Although she was daily on the phone with Aunt Meg, it was not until the third day that Meg had good news. Delia had passed all tests with flying colors. Terri was ecstatic, and when Mark Denton phoned that night, she responded with high good humor, "Of course I'd love to go out to dinner with you."

Later, seated at a secluded but elegant restaurant, he observed her as well as he could in the subdued candlelight. He had called her as soon as he returned from New York, planning to divert her or in some way relieve her distress. Now, as far as he could tell, there was no sign of distress. He was surprised, but fascinated by the sparkle of delight in those telling blue eyes, the way the dimple in the corner of her mouth danced in and out as, following his lead, she laughed and talked about nothing in particular.

"I take it," he finally said, "that your problem, whatever it was, has been satisfactorily resolved."

"Oh, yes. Yes, indeed. And I must thank you again," she said, flashing a grateful smile. "That time on your boat...just what I needed to bring me round. It was silly of me to worry so. And wrong." She chuckled. "As I told you, Angie's a bit way-out. She says your negative thoughts can damage someone, just as your positive thoughts can help them. I don't know if she's right, but, after that time on your boat, I began to think that everything was going to come out all right, and a few days later I got word that it had."

So, her problem had involved someone else. Someone not in this vicinity. A man? These thoughts and a sudden jolt of jealousy so distracted him that he lost track of what she was saying, and stared blankly at her question.

"Do you believe that?"

"Do I what?"

"Do you believe that you can make something come out right just by thinking it so?"

"Certainly not," he said with conviction.

"Well, I know it sounds unbelievable, but..." She regarded him in a thoughtful way, which for some reason he found disconcerting. "I have seen it happen," she said, almost in a whisper.

"Coincidence, very likely. Believe me, lady, it takes more than thinking to solve most problems. I've just returned from the United Nations session on peace talks in the Middle East and I wonder if anything can solve that problem."

"Oh, but that's just it. Don't you see? If someone would first visualize a practical, sensible compromise that pleases everyone instead of all that argument with both sides spouting about what they want." She began to quote from principal figures in the controversy, and he was surprised at her knowledge of the issues. "What really happened at this last session?" she asked.

His recounting of this led to a discussion of his column, and he was even more surprised at her knowledge of his work.

"You really do read me," he said, pleased.

"Oh, yes, I like the variety of your material, ranging from human-interest stories like that one about the little girl who had lost her kitten, to national and international affairs, which, thank you very much," she said, dimpling, "you always put in simple words that dummies like me can understand."

"You are no dummy," he asserted. He found it stimulating to talk to someone who made no attempt to flatter or quote in parrotlike fashion on every topic he had written. In fact, she strongly disagreed with some of his ideas and said so in no uncertain terms. So lively was their conversation that they lingered long over coffee and brandy, and were surprised when the waiter hovered near, indicating that the restaurant was closing. Once again, enraptured by Terri Thompson, he was completely unaware of the passage of time.

Regardless of the time, he was never completely unaware of her. He was haunted by thoughts of her when he was away, and so enlivened in her presence that he sought every opportunity to be with her. Although he had enjoyed more than a casual acquaintance with several women, now he seemed to have time for none but Terri. He took her to the theater, the

opera, to dine and dance, and on one sunny day
in the late fall, for a long sail on his boat.

A woman named Deedee Divine had faded
from his memory. Until the Saturday when he
was forcibly reminded of her. He had phoned to
invite Terri out for a late breakfast, and she suggested that instead she would fix breakfast at her
apartment. She said she was enjoying the quiet
while her chatterbox roommate was away. Angie
had found her soul mate, and was with him at a
weekend Life, Love, Living seminar.

Mark was glad they did not go out. He liked
being alone with her in the quiet apartment, a
fire crackling on the hearth, the rain beating
against the windows just as it had that night on
the boat. He liked the intimate atmosphere of
domesticity, with the early morning smells of
brewing coffee and frying bacon. The table was
prettily set, the bacon crisp, the waffles so light
and flaky they melted in his mouth, the coffee
hot and smoothly blended. Delicious.

And Terri... in a casual, loosely fitted but so
revealing pantsuit of soft peach velour, hair
tousled, her face void of makeup, so fresh and
vibrant that he could not take his eyes from her.

After breakfast, she brought out the chess-
board he had given her and placed it on the floor
before the fire. She had become rather pro-
ficient, but the three games he lost in rapid suc-
cession were not attributed to her skill, but to his
total absorption in her. The graceful movement
of slender fingers as she placed her pieces, the
clamp of pearly white teeth on her lower lip as

she contemplated her strategy, the mischievous sparkle in changeling blue eyes.

His breath caught when, after her third win, she lay back on the floor, practically howling with glee. "You should have seen yourself!" she choked. "That look on your face when I said checkmate!"

He hardly heard her. He was only conscious of the rise and fall of the small mounds of her breasts as she gasped with laughter. Under the soft peach fabric, as if set aflame by the blazing logs, her whole body shimmered, glowed and beckoned, a fiery invitation. In intuitive response, his mouth closed upon hers. Closed and clung. The sweet pressure of her lips in instant and hungry yielding ignited a flame of heat that surged though his body, bursting into an inferno of passion that burned and throbbed and ached for her. He wanted her, wanted to be inside her, to hear her cry out as he filled her need and his own. He did not hurry, but moved slowly, savoring the moment, the expectancy of fulfillment. He stretched beside her and pulled her to him, trailing kisses along her cheek, her neck and the throbbing hollow of her throat while his hands explored the exquisite contours of her body. He felt her fingers tangle in his hair, caress his face, linger tantalizingly at the base of his neck. His anticipation mounted, and he reveled in the eagerness of her response that begged, demanded and promised. Kindled by a desire he could hardly control, his hands and lips began a more intimate search, evoking from her a whisper of pure pleasure. Exultation, between love and lust, filled him, and he was overcome by the mounting pressure of his need. Now, in just a moment...

Abruptly, she pushed away from him and stood up.

What the hell! For a moment, he simply felt bereft. Something magical and wonderful, just within his reach, had been snatched away, cheating him. And her. She had been just as involved, as eager as he. So why...?

Shaken by fury and frustration, he stood up to face her. She backed away, held up a restraining hand. Damn! Did she think he was going to rape her?

"I'm sorry," she said. "It just isn't...not now. Not yet." Her eyes were penitent, wary. Those expressive blue eyes.

It was then he remembered Deedee Divine.

Remembered that first night he had seen her dance at Spike's. Her body undulating provocatively, an erotic flame fueled by the admiring crowd of leering onlookers. Those come-play-with-me eyes had teased, invited, promised. Cheated.

As Terri Thompson, those same blue eyes had lured him, tempted, promised. And now...

"What do you want from me, Terri Thompson?" His voice was harsh and husky, and he deliberately emphasized the name.

"N-nothing," she said hesitantly. "That is, friendship."

"Oh? I had the impression that we might share much more than friendship."

"But not now. Not yet," she repeated. "There are things... You don't know...that is, we haven't known each other very long."

His mouth twisted in a wry smile. "Not long, perhaps. But I thought we were beginning to know each other rather well."

She actually blushed! "I...oh, I know this may date me, but I don't take some things...very lightly."

He thought of Deedee Divine and the leering onlookers. Did she take him for a fool? He was assailed by a sudden thought. Was she trying to lure him into making a commitment, marriage, perhaps, before he discovered who she really was? He was ashamed of the thought. And angry. Only a few minutes ago he would have committed to anything she wished.

"Perhaps we need a cooling-off period," he suggested as he reached for his jacket.

Terri leaned against the door that had shut behind him, wanting to cry. Wanting to call him back, to beg him to take her in his arms and revive that wonderful, exhilarating eroticism of wanting and being wanted. She had never felt that way before, and the hardest thing she had ever done was to pull away, but when she gave herself to him, she wanted it to be with no lie standing between them. It was true that she did not take some things lightly. But the way she felt about Mark Denton was no light matter. She loved him.

This was ridiculous. She straightened and, trying to pull herself together, went to clear away the breakfast dishes. She couldn't be in love with a man she had known such a short time. And had met under such shameful circumstances.

That was the real problem. That first meeting and the fact that she had cheated him out of four hundred thousand dollars. That first meeting stood between them, no matter how close they had become during the past weeks.

Terri stood at the sink watching the water pour over the dish she was rinsing and thought about the way Mark had kissed her. He might not feel as deeply about her as she felt for him. But he liked her. As Terri Thompson. She liked his liking her and shrank from losing even that. Sometimes she thought he might understand if he knew the whole story. Several times she had been tempted to tell him, but each time had been checked by the sheer audacity of what she had done and the enormity of the sum. If it had been a hundred dollars, or even four thousand—repayable and forgivable, and they might have remained friends. But not with such a vast sum and her lie between them.

There had been times when she thought he suspected. Every now and then when he looked at her in a certain way or said something. But no. He was so blasé, so casual. Nobody could be casual about being cheated out of four hundred thousand dollars!

And now perhaps he felt Terri Thompson was a cheat, she thought disconsolately as she stacked dishes. Hearts do not really break, she told herself, but hers felt dead and leaden, as if all the recently found joy had been drained away. A cooling-off period. Did that mean she would not see him again?

She did see him, and after only a few days. If she had reservations, he told himself, he understood and would not rush her. In any case, he simply could not stay away. Who or whatever she was, she had totally bewitched him, and what he felt for her went deeper than erotic passion.

Knowing the trick she had pulled as a belly dancer, he had looked into Terri Thompson's eyes and seen honesty, sincerity and steadfastness. There were even moments when he had doubts. The glint of gold in her auburn hair when caught by the sun, the unruly lock she was forever pushing from her forehead. The color and curl of those luxuriant locks could never have been contrived from such straight black hair. There were wigs, of course. But the heavy black hair that swung gracefully over her shoulders had looked natural, too. Gracefully. That was it, he thought, smiling to himself. Funny how everything she did was done so gracefully. Moving chess pieces across the board, tugging at the string of her kite the day they flew kites in the park, or just the way she walked. Graceful, even as she stood swaying on the deck of his boat when it was buffeted by wind and waves. One night, when called upon to attend one of his mother's dinner parties, he had taken Terri with him.

"Such a delightful woman," his mother said later. "So poised among all those people she was just meeting. And so lively and gracious, she charmed everyone."

"Yes," he said, pleased. Even Uncle Jasper, he thought. He had watched intently when his mother introduced them—"My brother, Mr Goodrich"—and was almost sure he detected an awkwardness, a bit of shock. But, if so, she had instantly recovered, and stood up to Uncle Jasper's interrogation with a cool detached charm. "She is quite engaging."

His mother nodded. "Definitely a Tuesday child."

"Tuesday?" he asked, puzzled.

"Oh, you know," she said. "Tuesday's child is full of grace. She must have been born on a Tuesday."

"Oh." He was reminded that he didn't know when or where she had been born. Or who she was. Never mind the hair, there was no denying those eyes, that dimple and that melodious voice. No denying that she was the belly dancer who had enticed his young nephew, and who had lied to him.

But she was also Terri Thompson. A phrase from the poem imprinted itself on his mind. "Who's poised in her little world's center, and who is gentle, responsive, tender and true."

Responsive. By God, she was that, he thought, remembering how her responsiveness had excited his senses, triggered his sensuality to such a peak that he had almost lost control.

And true. Yes. He'd bet his life that Terri was true. There must be some explanation for what she had done. He had parted with Deedee Divine on such bad terms that of course Terri would be reluctant to expose herself. When they became closer, when she felt she could trust him, she would tell him, he hoped. In any event, he would wait.

CHAPTER EIGHT

BRIAN, Mark's leg man, looked up from the batch of newspapers and clippings that littered his desk. "We might want to check this out, Mark. That old controversy's brewing again."

Mark, perusing a printout just handed him by his secretary, did not glance up. It was the secretary, Ginger, a tall, attractive young woman with a deep brown complexion, who asked, "What controversy?"

"Big versus small business," Brain answered. "According to Sam Peterson, head of Allied Automobile Manufacturers, the State Commission on Economic Development would do well to examine its priorities. He claims an increase in tax exemptions would bring in well-established firms, generating more jobs and millions of dollars, overriding losses they have already sustained on loans to small business."

Ginger sniffed. "Chauvinist pig! Where does he get his statistics?"

Brian shot her an impish grin as he adjusted his glasses, folded one of the newspapers and began to read. "The record number of bankruptcies of State-sponsored small businesses is deplorable. Laxity in financing procedures at the Small Business Administration has landed business in the hands of inexperienced management, resulting in rapid failure or fraudulent practices as in the case of—"

"Oh, shut up. You just want to keep the economy where it has always been, in the hands of the white male big shots."

"Me? Don't point at me. I'm only quoting the experts."

Mark paid little heed to the discussion. He was accustomed to the good-natured squabbles between his blond, blue-eyed leg man and his peppy secretary who, compelled by race and sex, always entered the arena on the side of minorities. Mark scribbled a few notes on the paper and returned it to her. "Stick this sentence I've circled up here. And change this last line as indicated before you fax it out," he said.

"Okay, boss. But will you tell Mr Stupido here that one bad egg doesn't condemn the whole setup?"

"What bad egg and which setup?"

"She's talking about Eric Saunders," Brian said. "That guy who hoodwinked the Small Business Administration out of two hundred thousand dollars, which ain't exactly peanuts. And you can't say I'm against minorities, Ginger, 'cause Saunders is a white male."

"Oh, you're not panning him," Ginger declared. "You just want to shut up the whole agency on account of him."

"No, Miss Smarty. All I'm saying is that when an agency can be so easily bilked by a barefaced liar with a fake pottery plant, there's something rotten in the woodpile! And we better check it out, boss. Take a look," he added, laying several clippings on Mark's desk. Then he turned to Ginger. "Lunch time. Come on, you poor deprived female. I'll buy you a hamburger. What about you, boss?"

Mark, already scanning the clippings, shook his head. "You've given me my assignment. Guess I'll get to work." He waved the two out without looking up. Nothing newsworthy about this. Everybody knows the economy is flagging, and the State ought to boost any business, big or small, he thought, as he thumbed through the papers.

The thumb stopped, his interest perked by the case of Eric Saunders. Eric Saunders had received a loan, guaranteed by the State, of two hundred thousand dollars for his small business, a pottery plant. The plant turned out to be a fake and Saunders had absconded with the money, leaving the State as debtor and the small business agency on the carpet.

Mark got up from his desk and walked over to the window. From his fifth floor, he stared at San Francisco's busy Market Street and thought about it. Was the agency at fault? Laxity or complicity? Financing procedures for such loans were, or should be, rather strict, and unless there was someone on the inside who...

He stopped. He mustn't jump to conclusions, he thought, remembering something Nate had once said. "It's not words you love, buddy. It's power. The power of words."

Mark had bristled. "Meaning?"

"I mean you damn journalists can twist your words around a man's neck and hang him before he gets to trial. You consider yourselves judge and jury."

Mark had chafed at the implication. "Not true. We're observers for the public, and we owe it to our readers to present the facts." However, Nate's charges haunted, and try as he might, Mark could never dismiss them. Facts could be twisted, not always exposing the guilty or protecting the innocent. He might express an opinion, but never would he present a fact unless he knew without doubt that it was true. No easy task.

It was also true that words could be twisted. The nuance of a phrase or sentence could convey meaning, please or anger, inspire hate, joy, pity or pleasure. Yes, words were powerful, and one must be careful how facts were presented.

He studied the printed clippings. Saunders had taken the money and scrammed, so he did appear to be guilty. But Ginger was right, the agency shouldn't be condemned because of a single case. Or was there more? But if there was an accomplice...possible. He looked again at the clippings. The agency was holding a press conference tomorrow at ten, "To further acquaint the public of our services." Also, Mark thought, to defend itself against the allegations that were surfacing.

Mark checked his schedule. He would attend that conference.

*   *   *

Mark nodded at the reporters he knew and went over to sit by Sam Wells of the *Tribune*. They were deep in a discussion of the national Professional Golf Association playoff when officials from the small business agency filed in to take their seats on the podium. About to challenge Wells on his assertion that Watson didn't have a chance, Mark stopped in midsentence when he saw a woman take the seat on the right of the chairman. A woman wearing a chic coat dress of black gabardine, accentuated by a scarf that matched her striking blue eyes. A woman whose lovely face was capped by a mass of luxuriant golden curls. Terri Thompson.

What the hell was she doing here?

The chairman stood to greet the reporters and introduce his colleagues. Only one colleague registered with Mark, "Ms Terri Thompson, our chief loan officer."

Stunned, Mark tried to reconcile that high position with a belly dancer in a tawdry bar. What had Terri told him of her job?

Nothing much. As little as she had revealed of any phase of her life. Just that she worked for the State. He had pictured her in some menial clerk position, and had even, in trying to puzzle her out, seen her belly dancer stint as a supplement to her meager salary so she could afford that luxury condo she shared with Angie. That is, until she conned him, which was supplement enough.

Stop it, he cautioned himself, realizing that he was breathing hard. There must be some reason, some explanation for what she had done. Something that would exonerate her. Because that was what he wanted to believe. Only, he thought disconsolately, contrary to Angie's weird opinions, believing did not make it so.

Terri had seen him and nodded a smiling greeting. He returned the smile and nod, hoping his expression gave no indication of the conjectures whirling through his brain. Chief loan officer. A key position. Convenient for conspiracy in any financial scam. And anyone as devious as Ms Deedee Divine...

Mark heard not one word of the chairman's talk, none of the questions from reporters, no answers from participating officials. Nothing. Until the chairman summoned Terri to the mike. "Ms Terri Thompson, our chief loan officer, who came to us with excellent recommendations and a Master's degree in business from Stanford University. Ms Thompson is doing a superlative job and is here to explain our loan policy and procedures, and answer questions you might have."

She stood up and faced the audience. A Terri Thompson he had never seen before. Yes, he had seen her poised and serenely gracious. But never had he seen her look so competent, confident. Efficient. And, he thought, surprised, so composed. Didn't she know she was facing a roomful of barracudas, ready to eat her alive over the Saunders escapade?

She knew it. Inside she was quivering like a leaf. So much at stake—her reputation, her job, the very survival of the agency itself. Strangely enough, it was of none of these things she thought about as she forced an appearance of outer calm and gathered her wits for battle. She was thinking of the widow, Eliza Carr, whose stuffed animals were doing a booming mail order business with profits far beyond the support of her kids, and Joe Daniels, whose successful dance studio was bolstering his pride as well as his pocketbook. She thought of the applications on her desk, she thought of the waiting people, industrious people with ideas, talent, aspirations, needing a lift. Like a mother bear defending her cubs, Terri stood, ready to defend these people against the cloud of Eric Saunders.

She made no mention of Saunders in her talk. She focused on the positive. She talked about Eliza Carr and Joe Daniels. She detailed the activities of Sue and Anna Carroll, the sisters who had built a multimillion-dollar corporation from a small snowshoes business. She told of the enormity of their payroll, the sums spent for production materials from other California companies. She quoted statistics, small business successes, jobs generated, tax benefits. Lastly she talked of procedures, the careful screening of applicants, opportunities available through the agency.

But, however positive her presentation, the questions flung at her were negative and derisive. Skeptical when it was learned that she had been with the department only six months. "And yet you are the chief loan officer?"

She was prepared for this. "I inherited the position. I was hired as Mr Jason's assistant, and he left six weeks after my appointment."

"I see." The reporter in the gray suit had a strange glint in his eyes. "So you personally approved Mr Saunders's application."

"Of course. Along with several others." How could she forget? It was during that awful time when Mom got ill.

"Thank you." The man sat down, as if he had triumphantly proved a point.

A woman reporter waved her spectacles like a red flag. "When a loan is under consideration, do you personally inspect the business premises?"

"Not usually. Not always. Only when there is reason to doubt." And not even then, when she was working two jobs and worrying about Mom, she thought.

"Did you inspect Mr Saunders's pottery plant before you approved his loan?"

"No." Terri could not stem the hot flush that rose to her cheeks. She drew no comfort from the fact that she had never seen the place. Probably she would have been as impressed by the fake plant as John Drew. "It was inspected by another employee in whom I have every confidence."

The woman reporter's smile seemed more like a sneer. "I take it you also had every confidence in Mr Saunders's credit rating?"

"As did the bank in which he had on deposit matching funds for our guaranteed loan," she said.

The challenge was taken up by a man in shirt sleeves. "Did you inspect the credit rating of Larry Cobbs?" This question was met by chuckles, as this was one of Saunders's pseudonyms that had recently come to light.

Terri stiffened, but her answer was steady. "Certainly not. We were only concerned with an Eric Saunders."

Mark couldn't stand it. They were crucifying her. He wanted to get up, throw his arms around her and defend her against the reporters who had found a ready target for their accusations. She was so vulnerable. So—so...

Guilty? What kind of fool are you, Mark Denton? When you know what she is. This whole thing could be a setup, carefully planned between two people who switched names and identities as easily as they changed clothes. The matching fund, the two hundred thousand dollars deposited by Saunders could have been part of what was bilked from him by one Deedee Divine, who had probably posed as a belly dancer for just such a purpose. Otherwise why would a woman with a master's in business be dancing?

Ha! Credentials, like a pottery plant, could be faked.

She didn't look like a fake. He couldn't help a little glow of pride as he watched her volley with the reporters. Exuding a certain dignity, she replied to their questions quickly and precisely, a woman well versed in the field of business. If she was a fake, she was a damn good one.

As good as she had been a belly dancer.

He was reminded that all con artists were good in whatever guise they assumed. How else could they convince anyone to buy their story? As Terri was now convincing the reporters, except for Sally Eastern from the *Chronicle*, who kept defiantly waving her glasses as if she didn't believe a word. If Sally knew what he knew...

Well, what did he know, damn it? There might be some reason...

Fascinated, he watched Terri Thompson manage her audience. Before the conference was over, she had them in her corner. Yes, the Eric Saunders case was an aberration, clearly a fraud, well planned in advance. The agency had been caught off guard and she must shoulder the blame. A tragic mistake, but also a warning. Applicants would be more carefully screened than ever before. But the agency must be preserved. The agency's services must remain open and available to the deserving. She welcomed public participation and invited them to visit the office. No, loan applications, past or present, were not open for inspection. Privacy of clients must be protected. But businesses were always open to the public, and she would be glad to arrange a tour for any person or group.

She took her seat and the chairman rose to second her invitation and close the meeting.

There was the usual hubbub after a press conference. Some rushing out with their pads or recorders, others stopping to converse, still others moving toward the front to make some comment or elicit more information from the agency people. Mark noticed that several men converged upon Terri. Sam Wells, dapper and a well-known ladies' man, had leaped from his seat and gone straight to her. Mark saw him bend toward her and say something, watched Terri smile and nod, her blue eyes twinkling in that special playful way. A hot burst of fury exploded within him, burning and sizzling through his veins. That smile, that teasing come-play-with-me invitation... She had no right!

And if you, Sam Wells, knew her... If you knew that she is a deceitful, conniving con woman... Maybe he ought to tell him. Or make her tell. Just go up, take her by the shoulders and shake her until she confessed to everyone that she was a cheating, lying, deceitful, conniving...

He had reached her and she stretched out a hand. "Hello, Mark. I was so surprised. I had no idea you would be here."

Now the smile focused on him, melting him. "Hi, Terri. How about lunch?"

CHAPTER NINE

MARK took Terri's arm in a possessive grasp, expertly evading her admirers, and led her from the building.

"I was impressed," he said when they reached the sidewalk.

"Were you? Really?" she asked.

"Oh, yes, you gave quite a performance." A damn good performance, he thought, unable to quell his suspicions.

"I was so nervous, but... You think it came across all right? That we'll get good press coverage?"

"Definitely. They swallowed everything you said."

She seemed not to notice the snide innuendo. "I don't know. That reporter that kept waving her red-rimmed glasses at me seemed so doubtful. Who is she?"

"Sally Eastern, from the *Chronicle*," he said. A woman, he thought, not so easily turned on by another woman's beautiful face, or the musical sincerity of her voice. "Don't worry about her. You were most appealing... quite believable."

"I'm glad." She sighed. "This Saunders episode was quite a threat."

"Yes. Left you in quite a spot, didn't it? Might have opened up a whole can of worms."

"Well, yes. I suppose," she said thoughtfully. "Only it really is an isolated and quite unprecedented incident." She spoke with such candor that he wondered why he continued this one-sided sparring. Why didn't he confront her, bring everything into the open and have it out with her once and for all? "I was really scared this morning. Mr Anderson, my boss, wanted me to carry the ball and I felt there was so much at stake, you see." She looked anxiously at him and he knew why he didn't want to bring anything into the open. Because his suspicions might be confirmed, and he didn't want that. All he wanted to do was take that innocent upturned face in his hands and kiss that inviting mouth. Right here in the middle of all the traffic and milling crowd of people surrounding them. To hell with them and to hell with his plaguing doubts.

She stopped. "Look, I don't have much time. I have to get back to work. There's a bistro around the corner where we might get a quick salad. Okay?"

"Okay." Anywhere as long as she was with him.

Seated in the bistro, she neglected her salad as she continued her spiel on the agency. "It's so important, you see. Amazing, the people who come to us. You wouldn't believe the new and exciting projects that are out there. It would be a shame to miss out on them. I do hope the journalists got the right message. We are on the spot now and we need the support of the press.''

He nodded, listening. Was this a message for him? Because he was one of those journalists she wished to coerce? She had never talked about her job before. All those times he had seen her, and he had not even known she was with the State Commission on Economic Development, much less chief loan officer. She had never mentioned her job. Not one damn word.

And now she was talking her head off.

Because he had discovered where she worked and might make connections and damaging conclusions?

Oh, hell, she didn't know that he knew who she was. He was certain of that.

''You're being very quiet, Mr Denton,'' she said, twinkling at him in that special way. Just as she had at Sam Wells, damn it! ''What are you going to say about this morning's conference, or aren't you telling?''

''Nothing. That is, I don't know.'' Damn, he was babbling like an idiot. No, like a besotted fool, putty in the hands of a conniving witch.

Certainly not an investigating journalist. What about his responsibility to the public? What about getting the facts?

He was glad when lunch was over. When he got away from her, maybe he could think.

But when she got up to rush to her office, he reached for her hand, wanting to detain her.

"Let go, mister. I got no time to dream and drift," she said, dimpling. "I got a heavy load to lift."

He laughed. "All those heavy applications?"

"Right. And what about you? Don't you have some heavy matters to pontificate on? Some revolution or military coup? Or maybe," she added, suggestively, "some important press conference?"

"Okay, okay," he said, but he did not release her hand. She was a tease and a joy. "How about Sunday? We could drive up to Tahoe."

She said she was sorry, she was leaving for Seattle Friday and wouldn't be back until late Sunday. He let her go, wondering what in the hell was in Seattle.

Even on the plane to Seattle, Terri could think of nothing but Mark Denton. He was really an enigma to her. He always appeared so carefree, casual, no matter what he was doing, dancing, playing chess or just standing on his boat in a pair of faded jeans, stirring a pot of soup. Living life with a light touch. One would never believe he was the dedicated journalist, reporting from on-the-spot revolutions and shotgun elections in Timbuctoo or wherever. She devoured his columns, as engrossed in what he said as in what he was...a tall, handsome, carefree man with black, always unruly hair, a smile that started at the corners of his mouth and spread, brightening his face and eyes. Dark, deep-set eyes that regarded her with such intensity that sometimes she felt he was trying to burrow into her soul.

"You live in Seattle?" inquired the man sitting next to her.

"No, just visiting," she replied, pretending to be absorbed in the magazine open on her lap. She didn't want to talk to a stranger. She wanted to think about Mark. She liked the way he talked to her, listened to her, with total concentration. And when he kissed her... She closed her eyes, remembering. Feeling her body melt and respond to the tender, passionate demand of his lips, feeling her body spring to life at his touch. She ached for him, ached to be in his arms, ached to surrender herself to the hungry, exciting, erotic yearnings evoked by his touch, the feel of his body against hers. She wanted...

She sat up, turned a page of the magazine and stared down at it. What was she going to do about Mark? When could she tell him?

She couldn't tell him. There were so many others involved. Her mother. Mom might have had a hard life, danced in places Terri would not have dreamed she would enter. Yes, Spike's Bar had been an eye-opener, revealing much she had never known about Delia. But she did know that Delia was not a cheat. She was a decent, honest, straightforward woman who would never forgive a despicable, devious caper that had conned a man out of such a monstrous sum.

So she had lied to Mom, too. A kind, benevolent benefactor, Jasper Goodrich.

Oh, Lord! Jasper Goodrich. How had she managed not to faint right there in the middle of Mark's mother's party when Mrs Denton said, "My dear, I want you to meet my brother, Mr Goodrich." It had been all she could do to keep her composure, smile and take his hand when she must have been blushing with shame. If he knew that she was Deedee Divine...

If her mother knew what she had done...

If Mark knew. And he would know if he ever met her mother. She could hear open, honest Delia saying with perfect frankness, "I'm a dancer. Yes, I bet I've danced my way across the continent many times over." She would laugh and talk and he would ask. And he would know.

Mark and her mother must never meet. Maybe she should look for another job, move far away from San Francisco. She loved her job. She loved Mark.

She had ruined her life in a mess of lies.

Mom looked beautiful. Positively radiant. "I feel wonderful, Terri!"

"I'm so glad," Terri said, hugging her. This was worth a million lies.

"The doctors want me near for a few more months. But they see no complications and are amazed at my rapid progress. I must write Mr...what's his name? Goodlaw? If it hadn't been for him—"

"Oh, Mom, people like that don't correspond with everyone they give money to."

"Don't they?" Delia looked puzzled. "I should think they'd be happy to know what their kindness means to someone else. Of course, I know he didn't answer my first letter, but—"

"Mom! He probably never saw it. People like that are surrounded by secretaries, accountants and...tax lawyers. Nine times out of ten they don't know where their money went."

"I don't believe that. I think he'd like to know what a miracle it did for me. And I'm going to write him."

"All right, Mom. If it makes you feel better. I'll mail it." One more lie. She changed the subject, talked about Angie and the new apartment.

"What about your social life?" Aunt Mary asked. "Any new men?"

"Not many," she answered. Only one. And she certainly didn't want to talk about him. She changed the subject again. She talked about her job and her interesting clients.

Her mother was particularly interested in Joe Daniels's dance studio. "Maybe I could get a job there."

"Mom, you don't need to ever work again."

"Dancing isn't work. And teaching would be a piece of cake. Not like tramping the boards everywhere."

"We'll see." She changed the subject again. Told them about the Saunders episode and the press conference. Remembered that Mark had not written about it. Not one word. She wondered why.

*   *   *

` Don't like to make a statement until I get the facts," Mark said to Brian. "Anything more surfaced on Eric Saunders, alias Larry Cobbs?"

"Nothing but a whole bunch of other aliases."

"Check 'em out."

Brian's brows went up. "All of them?"

"How the hell else could you check him out? Certainly all of them."

"Gonna take a lot of leg work, boss."

"So? That's what you're paid for, isn't it?"

Brian was somewhat taken aback. Wasn't like the boss man to snap. Wasn't like him to follow up on small-potato leads, either. But... "Right. I'll get on it pronto," he said, seizing his briefcase and departing. Mine not to reason why, he thought. But he sure wondered why the fuss over a relatively unimportant matter, and why the boss had been in such a hell of a mood lately.

Left alone, Mark moved restlessly about the office, stared with unseeing eyes out of the window. Strange. Women had come and gone out of his life, and he had never cast a backward glance. Until Terri Thompson. He couldn't let her go. Couldn't stop thinking about her. A woman who had bilked him out of... He stopped, knowing that he would give all he had already given her, and more, to know that she was not what she might be. A liar, a cheat, an inveterate con artist. He had to know.

Even so, he could not bear to put a tracer on her. He had no such qualms about tracing Eric Saunders. If there was any connection between him and Terry, he would... What? What would he do?

He didn't want to think about that. But he had to know. Maybe then he could think of something else, could get on with his work. Meanwhile—well, thank goodness he was several weeks ahead with his columns.

He picked up the phone and called Terri at her office, gave his name and waited for her secretary to transfer the call, reveled in the sound of her voice, her obvious pleasure in his call. "Mark. How are you and what's on your mind?"

"Thought I'd like to take you up on that offer of a tour."

"Oho! So you mean to check on us before you write about us."

So she had been waiting for his comments. "My usual procedure. Do you mind?"

"Of course not. I'm delighted. Let me know your preferred time and I'll arrange a tour that will fit in with your schedule. And I'll try to stick to this vicinity. You know we're scattered all over the state."

"I don't care about the vicinity," he said. "And I don't want you to arrange a tour. I want you to take me, if possible, to several businesses whose loans have been processed through you." Was he being too blunt? Would she be suspicious? "Is that possible?"

"Well, yes." She laughed, as if not at all perturbed. "A little unusual, but certainly possible for such an important columnist as Mark Denton.

And, to tell the truth, I do have my favorites. Let me check my schedule and get back to you.''

She got back in touch the very next day with a list of local businesses and within a very few days, they started their inspections.

He found that she really did have her favorites. Mostly really small businesses that had been launched with very small loans. The first place Terri took him was to an old house in Oakland. It wasn't exactly a disreputable area, but it certainly was not the most ideal. Mostly residential, with some pretty, well-kept houses adjacent to veritable shacks. A convenience store, a bar, a seedy restaurant. Children roaming the streets or peering over fences. Terri parked behind a van in the driveway and rang the bell of the two-story house. The door was opened by a woman with stringy rather disheveled red hair and a cigarette dangling from her mouth.

''Ms Thompson,'' she cried, obviously glad to see Terri. ''We're just doing the pasteup for this month's issue. Wanna see it?''

''That's what we came for,'' said Terri. ''I know you're busy but I do hope you have time to tell Mr Mark Denton about your business. You might get a bit of publicity from his syndicated column. Mark, this is Vera Cox, who publishes a monthly magazine.'' Terri's teasing smile flashed. ''I thought you might like to see how it's done.''

Mrs Cox took the cigarette out of her mouth and extended her hand. ''Pleased to meet you,'' she said. ''Come on back and take a look at what's going on and then we can go in the front room to talk." She banished two small children. "I told you to stay out there in the backyard until I called you for lunch. Now get!" The children, fortified by licorice sticks from Terri's purse, disappeared, and Mrs Cox led them into a large room at the back of the house. A room that had a kind of disorderly order about it, and smelled of paste and paper. There were two computers, not in use at the moment, a man seated at a desk talking into one of three telephones, and two women cutting and pasting at two long tables.

"We have the columns off the computers," Mrs Cox explained. "And they are arranging the columns and ads to ready the pages for the printer." She picked up one of the finished pages to show him. It contained two articles, one on safety precautions for bicyclers, one on menus for Thanksgiving. There were two ads, one for a children's shoe store and one from a grocery store.

"Very well done," he said before she led him to the front room where Terri suggested, "Tell Mr Denton how you got started."

"Out of necessity," said Mrs Cox, lighting another cigarette and apologizing, "Sorry. I know it's bad for me but I can't seem to do without them." She drew on it and then began. "It was tough going after Ken died. The welfare checks were not nearly enough, and downright humiliating, you know. I didn't want to leave the children so I got the idea for a local magazine. Ken used to work for a newspaper, you see, and

I knew the income came from ads." She explained how, starting out on her own with just a typewriter, she began to write articles of interest to housewives and have several copies made. "Just one or two pages at first. Me and the children would clip them together, fold them and pile them into little Kenny's wagon. Lord, we must have walked for miles to leave the pamphlets on as many doorsteps as we could," she said, choking a little on her cigarette as she laughed. Armed with a long list of nonpaying "subscribers", she began to collect ads from local businesses, "Which did pay," she said. "But not enough to get me off welfare for quite a while, since I had to use some of my welfare money to buy supplies and pay for the copying."

She explained that the whole operation just got bigger and bigger. And somebody told her about the Small Business Administration. "I met Ms Thompson," she said, giving Terri a grateful smile. "Cause that first loan officer that came out here wouldn't give me the time of day. If it hadn't been for Ms Thompson..." The loan guaranteed by the agency had purchased supplies and starting capital to hire helpers. "I got two ad men, and a computer operator and those women you saw who do the pasting, and several boys who deliver the still free magazine, only now it's a six-page newspaper with enough ads to pay the overhead and get me and the children a long way from welfare. And oh, yes, I got several writers. I just pay twenty-five dollars for an article, but you'd be surprised how many writers

we have in this area that would just like to see
their words in print,'' she said, smashing out her
cigarette. ''Anyway, sometimes these articles get
picked up by bigger, better-paying publications,
and they luck out that way. Yes, sir, I got a good
business going, and if it hadn't been for Ms
Thompson I might still be supplementing it with
welfare. Right, Ms Thompson?''

''Wrong,'' said Terri. ''With your ideas and
your energy, you'd have made it by yourself
eventually. We just primed the pump and in-
creased the pace. No telling where you'll go from
here.''

The next call they made was not too far away
from the first. Another large house, newly
painted, with play equipment in the yard. This
time they were greeted by an elderly black
woman.

''Mrs Mary Ables,'' said Terri. ''Mrs Ables,
this is Mark Denton, who is very interested in
your day-care facility.''

Mrs Ables, who seemed quite spry despite her
weight and gray hair, very graciously showed him
over the place. The house had obviously been re-
modeled to accommodate children. Walls removed to make more space, small chairs and
tables, pint-size toilet facilities and wash basins.
The whole place brightly painted and cheerful.
Several children, supervised by two younger
women, were happily engaged with books,
coloring crayons and toys.

''Mrs Ables was also on welfare,'' Terri explained when they left. ''A grandmother saddled

with three grandchildren. She just marched into the office one day saying that anybody raising anybody else's kids was running a business and what could we do for hers.'' Terri burst into laughter. ''She was quite adamant. When we told her she needed matching funds, she put up her house, which was clear even if it was falling down about her and needed new wiring and plumbing. Anyway, we just couldn't get rid of her, and you see the result.''

''I'm thinking it was you that wouldn't be rid of her,'' he said. ''Isn't she rather over the age to receive a loan, and do all your clients come from welfare?''

She wrinkled her nose at him. ''Okay, so I had to pull a few strings. But wouldn't you rather have her off welfare and paying taxes? And isn't she running a great place?''

He admitted that all this was true.

''Now I'm going to take you to a place where you might classify the loan recipients under age,'' she told him.

This facility proved to be well out of town. A community of old farms, which were gradually being taken over by developers.

''Kinda sad,'' Terri remarked. ''To see good fertile earth covered by concrete.''

''Yes,'' he said. ''But I guess these little farms can't compete with the big commercial ones.''

''Well, I'm taking you to a farm that's holding on. And you'll be surprised at how that's being managed.''

He was surprised. Quite astonished when she drove into a farmyard filled with old and new automobiles and one or two tractors. Well, not exactly filled. Maybe ten cars parked around a barn, which had been converted into a garage.

"This is Keith Johnson," Terri said, when a lanky, freckle-faced boy approached them. He can't be twenty-one, Mark thought, as the boy wiped a grease-stained hand on his pants, but, thank goodness, didn't extend it. "This is Mr Denton, Keith. He's a friend of mine. He is interested in your operation and would like to look it over."

"Sure, Miss Thompson." Keith, who also seemed well acquainted with Terri, grinned. "Any friend of yours is a friend of ours."

They had parked some way from the barn, and as they walked toward it, Terri told him about Keith. "This is a very smart young man," she said. "He says he never did like farm work, but loved to tinker with machinery. Always kept the family tractor in order. He was working at a garage in Vallejo, but wasn't making much money. When his father died, he used the insurance money to match funds for a loan and opened his business right here on the old family property."

It seemed to be a flourishing business. A large area around the barn was paved and accommodated the vehicles that did not fit into the barn. The barn itself was well equipped with the usual lifts and pulleys, as well as storage space for

needed tools. Two other boys, who looked even
younger than Keith, looked up from the engine
they were working on to call a greeting to Terri.
The two girls, who he was sure were still in their
teens, also seemed to know her. They were
working in the well-lighted, well-equipped office,
originally the hayloft at the back of the barn.
"Man, I can punch the you-know-what out of
these keys now," one of them said to Terri.
"Bookkeeping is a piece of cake since I went to
that computer class you told me about. Look
here, let me show you."

Mark watched Terri as she talked with the girl,
listening, encouraging. Just as she had stopped
to kid one of those boys downstairs about his
earring. It occurred to him that she was perfectly
at ease with these kids, just as she had been with
the older Mrs Ables and the rather coarse Mrs
Cox. Terri had...what had his mother said? Yes.
Grace. And it was real. No facade. The kind of
grace that made her accept people for what they
were and extend an understanding kindliness, a
certain dignity and graciousness that she had
exuded even among those men at Spike's Bar.

The memory of Spike's made him irritable.
When they left and Terri asked what he thought
of the operation, he said he thought Keith awfully
young to be trusted with that kind of
responsibility.

She said Keith was twenty-three, two years
older than the required age.

He said that guy with the earring strongly resembled one he had caught stealing his hubcaps a few months before.

She chuckled. "Well, now he isn't. But if he were, wouldn't you be glad to see him working instead of stealing?"

CHAPTER TEN

MARK walked rapidly, invigorated by the crisp, cool morning air. He always walked to work from his Nob Hill apartment. A steep incline, downhill all the way, but easier than maneuvering his Jaguar through the heavy traffic. Anyway, it was good exercise and gave him time to think. There were times he had drafted a whole column in his mind while he walked.

Not now, though. Not when all he could think about was Terri Thompson. She must be as deep as Angie in that supernatural metaphysical voodoo stuff. She had sure as hell put a spell on him. All the facts screamed guilty! Yet, one look at her and he was ready to fall on his knees and forgive all.

Could she really be a fake? She had moved so easily around each one of those people yesterday, shedding "the lustre of purity, goodness, and grace". Damn! Why did he keep relating her to that poem? But it was true. She approached all kinds of people with such concern, such grace. She—

"Oh! Sorry," he muttered, managing to catch the woman he had bumped into before she fell backward.

She was not grateful. "You don't own these streets, buster! Think nobody got rights but big fat no-tax-paying creeps like you?"

"Sorry," he said again, retrieving one of her overloaded bags of refundables that had fallen and handing it to her.

She leaned closer, reeking of tobacco, stale whiskey and sweat. "I got rights same as you!"

"Right." He stepped a little away, conscious of the amused glances of other walkers.

"Ought to have more respect for a woman old enough to be your ma! Ought to be sorry for a poor old soul who needs."

He was sorry for her. He found a ten dollar bill and handed it to her. She'd probably spend it on more wine, but what else could he do?

The surprised woman greedily thrust the bill into her bosom and grinned at him through stained teeth. "Thankee, son. The Lord loves a cheerful giver. The Lord will bless you," she murmured as she trudged up the hill, melting into the crowd.

He wondered about that as he walked on. Was he a cheerful giver? Nate made the usual yearly charitable donations for him—a hospital in Tanzania, some children's home and that place for the homeless. Tax shelters? Maybe the old woman was right. Yes, a few handouts to street people. But I'm not personally involved, like Terri, he thought, who chatted easily with the drinkers at a bar or those teenagers in that converted barn. He wasn't that kind of giver.

He didn't think of the time he had pulled a child from a burning house during the fighting in El Salvador, or how, under gunfire, he had once delivered wheat to starving people, caught in the midst of civil strife. Routine episodes in the life of a journalist, he would have said, had he thought about them at all. Instinctive, not cheerful giving.

And, cynic that he was, doubts about Terri continued to plague him. Had she deliberately steered him toward the smaller businesses, those that had elicited loans not big enough to steal? Owners who would evoke sympathy, not suspicion.

He was not thinking straight. Any flourishing business, big or small, was...well, flourishing. Nobody had absconded with the seed money. And if there were plans for future frauds...

Now he was being stupid. Con artists didn't stick around to pull another scam in the same place. They moved on.

Terri wasn't moving. She seemed very interested and deeply immersed in her job. The thought brightened his mood. His steps were buoyant as he entered his office. "Hi, Ginger. Brian. Anything new on Saunders?"

"Another wife. In Virginia."

"Another? There was no mention of a wife being involved."

"Oh, she wasn't. She had only been married to him for four months and was as surprised as the agency when he disappeared. Seems she was also bilked out of whatever she had."

"And there's another wife in Virginia?" Not Terri, he thought. She was right here.

"Not exactly a wife. Just one of the many women Eric Saunders married and bilked. That was his mode of operation," Brian said as he went to his desk and pulled out his chair.

"Oh?"

"Yeah, he's left a whole string of broken hearts. He seems to have quite an appeal for the ladies."

Like Terri appealed to men? Was that her mode of operation?

"Something else came up," Brian said, leaning back in his chair. "A little late, though, and not much help. Seems he was seen in Seattle a few weeks ago, but managed to elude capture."

Seattle. That rang a bell.

She had thought about it ever since she left Seattle. There was no other way. She had to leave town. And she had to do it before Mom fully recuperated, moved here, met Mark and everything came out, exploding like a bomb in her face.

Too many people. Mom, who would never condone the price Terri had paid for her life. Mom, who had been told she borrowed the money, was forever singing praises of her benefactor. And if Mark, or anyone, should mention the name of Jasper Goodrich, or if, heaven forbid, Mom ever met him, which she certainly might if Terri continued to see Mark...

Jasper Goodrich, who had his own conception about the caliber of belly dancers, and whose conception would not be raised when he found out what one particular belly dancer had done to cheat him out of more money than she could ever possibly repay. Money ostensibly paid to save his grandson from the manipulations of that same belly dancer. So what would he think of his nephew being involved with her? If he knew that Mark...

Mark. How could she ever tell him? At first she had thought he might have recognized her. But no. She was sure now that he fully accepted her as Terri Thompson. His manner toward her was so open, so accepting, so...admiring? He was spending more and more time with her. Heavenly times, no matter what they did. Sailing on his boat, playing chess, teasing Angie or just sitting together, talking, arguing. And when he kissed her... Terri felt her body respond even as she sat at her desk.

She got up, walked over to the water cooler and took a long drink. This was not the time to indulge in blissful memories. She had to think.

She could tell Mark.

Oh, sure... "Look, there's something I need to tell you. I'm really Terri Thompson, but I did meet you once before and you thought I was Deedee Divine, which I was, only..."

Terri dropped the paper cup as she imagined the look on Mark's face as it was that night, glaring down at Deedee Divine. She got some paper towels, mopped up the water as she saw herself, trying to explain. "Kinda complicated. My mother was sick and..."

"Goodness, Terri. What happened?" Liz, one of the loan officers, began to help, mopping water from her dress. "Messed yourself up, kid. But it's okay. Only water. No spots. Terri, I want you to take a look at this application."

"Sure." Terri went to her desk, sat down with Liz, absorbed herself totally in the work at hand.

But, whenever she was alone, she could think of nothing but her dilemma. There was too much to explain to too many people. She really liked Mark Denton. He liked her—might be falling in love with her, and she could not bear to see that love change to hate. If she should go away, never see him again... The only way to uncomplicate her life was to leave town.

Leave her new job? She liked what she was doing. And finding another job would not be easy. But she had to keep working, had to pay the bills, provide a place for her mother.

Diligently, Terri set out to do what she had to do. She sent out applications and references to places far from California.

She spoke of her plans to no one but Angie, pledging her to secrecy. "I don't want the agency folks to know I'm leaving this job till I get another one." Angie was surprised, and very put out, as Terri knew she would be.

But she had to tell her. She knew Angie counted on her to share the expenses of the condo, and if she suddenly moved... And that was how she planned to do it. Quickly, before Mark could ask questions.

* * *

It jumped out at him that very night when, on impulse, he dropped by the condo to see Terri. Impulse, indeed! When wasn't he trying to see her?

Terri took his jacket and stopped to pay the paperboy. Mark went into the living room to find Angie, on one of her rare nights at home, seated on the floor, poring over a batch of charts.

"Mark!" she said, "I'm glad you dropped by. I want you to talk to Terri."

"Oh?"

"About her plans to move."

"Move?" He gave a start. "From this apartment?"

"From this apartment, her job, the whole darn city."

His heart pounded with a dreadful suspicion. A con artist leaving the arena? "Where's she going?"

"Hasn't made up her mind about that." Angie spread her hands. "Ain't that a kick? Not to anywhere. Just away."

He stared at her, sick with apprehension. "Why?"

"That's what I'm trying to find out now." Angie bent over her charts. "All I know is she comes back from Seattle announcing she might be moving on and I should be looking out for another roommate."

Seattle. All those trips to Seattle. That time he found her soaked by the rain, not knowing whether she was coming or going, something awful pressing on her mind. Was that when

Saunders had been sighted in Seattle? She had bounced right back. When he got away free and clear?

Angie looked at him. "She didn't tell you?"

"No." Not one damn word.

Terri, who had been hanging up his jacket, came into the room. "How about a drink, Mark? A martini, or would you rather a hot cup of coffee? I was thinking of making a pot."

He started to shake his head, then changed his mind. "Coffee sounds good," he said. While she made it, he might elicit more information from Angie.

Terri went into the kitchen and Mark joined Angie on the floor. "You have no idea why she plans to move?"

"None. No indications in her horoscope, either." She tapped the papers idly, a puzzled expression on her face. "I don't understand it. She's mad about her job, and I think she's got a case on you. Maybe..." She shot a piercing glance at him. "What are you?"

"Huh? Oh. I'm a writer."

"I know that. What's your sign?"

"Sign?"

Angie's lips tightened with exasperation. "Birth sign. When were you born?"

"Oh. July six, nineteen—"

"Cancer! Yes, of course. I should have known. You have the personality and all the qualities. A perfect match for a Sagittarian. That's Terri's sign. So that shouldn't be a problem," she said, looking more puzzled. "Rich, too, aren't you?"

He nodded. "Relatively."

"Not that that would matter to a Sagittarian."

"Oh?" Might not matter to a Sagittarian, he thought. But it sure would matter to a woman who had helped herself to four hundred thousand of his dollars! He was getting fed up with this irrelevant talk about signs. He leaned toward her. "Look, Angie, this was rather sudden, wasn't it? Surely there must have been some indication before now."

"None, I tell you. And there's nothing here, either."

He wanted to shake her. What the hell did she expect to find in those papers she kept tapping? "Look, she must have said something."

Angie wasn't listening. "If I had the exact hour and minute of her birth," she mused. "Terri doesn't know that, and that's so important. You see—" she leaned toward him to confide "—nothing can dim the brilliance of the sun when it is in a sign. And, when Terri was born, it was in Sagittarius. But there are other factors to consider. In addition to the sun and moon, the two luminaries, the planets also affect your life, according to the sign they were in when you were born, their exact location in the sky, distance from each other by degree, aspect and so forth."

He nodded. He didn't know what she was talking about. Didn't care. Terri. Getting away?

Angie explained, "You see, the sun might have been in the zodiac sign of, let us say, Gemini, so of course you are a Gemini with those basic characteristics. But the moon, ruling your emotions, might have been in Aries, so your love life is influenced by Aries qualities. Pluto, ruling the mind, could have been in some crazy sign that messes up your mental processes. See?''

He saw he wasn't getting anywhere with this looney tune and was glad when Terri came in bearing a tray. He got up to help her set the coffee and some luscious looking pastries on the coffee table. He wasn't hungry.

He frowned at Terri. ''You're thinking of moving away?''

She shot an exasperated look at Angie, then turned to him. ''Nothing definite.'' Did she look a little wary? ''I just wanted to let Angie know, in case. She could be looking around for someone else to share the condo.''

Angie looked up. ''Ain't that a kick!'' She shook her head. ''We've been here just two months, all settled in, and now she's ready to blow. Just like a Sagittarian! Careless. Too busy finding causes to cherish and defend to look where she's going every minute or worry about whose toes she's stepping on.''

''Angie, will you stop it?''

''I will not stop it. It's my toes you're stepping on and you don't even know where you're going and I don't see any cause. Why this sudden departure?''

''I'm not suddenly departing! I only said I...I might make a move.'' She wished she hadn't said anything at all. Only she had to. She didn't see any way out of her dilemma but to move away, and she didn't want to leave Angie in the lurch.

"Anyway," she said, "I'm not leaving now. So can't we just drop it?"

But Angie wouldn't drop it. She kept grumbling about the unpredictable quirks of nature in some people and how Terri might have been deviously affected by her ascendant, the sign rising on the eastern horizon at the exact moment of her birth. Terri wished she would shut up.

She wished Mark would say something. "Your coffee's getting cold," she reminded him. "And don't you want one of these apricot tarts? They're awfully good. I got them from that bakery next to the deli."

He stared at the tarts, then at her. Stood up. "Let's get out of here."

She hesitated, half afraid. He looked positively menacing. He strode out into the hall and she willed herself to follow. Silently he got into his jacket, took down one of hers and held it for her. Hardly waiting for her to struggle into it, he clamped a hand on her arm and propelled her out into the night. Like the night he had propelled her into a booth at Spike's. "You lied to me!" Her knees felt weak as the dreadful premonition seized her. He knows. He knows. She wanted to break away, run, hide. She wanted to clutch his arm, explain, beg him to understand.

But her mouth was dry, and he had a firm grip on her elbow. All she could do was stumble along beside him, almost running, two steps to his long one.

Finally he spoke, never breaking his stride. "I thought we were friends."

"We... we are," she panted. Maybe he didn't know.

"So why all the secrecy?"

"Secrecy?"

"About moving. Were you planning to sneak away? Just disappear into thin air?"

"I—no." She stopped. Because that was just what she planned to do. Disappear. So he would never know.

"Well?" His bark startled her so that she really did stumble, falling on her knees to the grass. Where was he headed, she wondered, as he caught her up in a strong, unloving grasp, and hurried her along. "Well?" he said again. "Why didn't you tell me you're moving?"

"But I'm not. I was just... just planning—"

"Moving, planning, what's the difference?" He picked her up and swung her onto the deck of his boat before she realized they had crossed the wharf. He pushed her ahead of him into the cabin, shut the door and switched on a light. Faced her. "Don't you think it's time you came clean with me?"

She couldn't speak. She could only stare into his face, dark as a thundercloud, the furious, penetrating eyes boring into her just as they had that time in the bar. "Took me in, didn't you... lying, conniving, double-dealing cheat... legal restitution, you know... jail..." Chilled to the bone, she drew her jacket closer, a shield against his wrath.

Mark couldn't stand it. The guilt in that sweet, innocent face, the quiver in those soft lips, eyes that laughed and teased now wide with fright. Terri, so small and vulnerable, helpless, huddled in her jacket like a trapped animal. His heart turned over and he felt his defenses crumble.

"You're cold," he said, and turned to switch on the heat. His anger faded and he realized he was as scared as she. How many other devious schemes had Saunders, with his damnable appeal, involved her in? He turned to Terri. "He isn't worth it, you know."

"Who?"

"That guy you're ready to follow to hell and back."

There was nothing fake about the amazement in her face. "Who—what are you talking about?"

Could he be wrong? Could there really be two such look-alikes in the world? Could the woman before him have no connection with a barroom belly dancer, and a perfectly legitimate reason for wanting to move? The possibility so relieved and cheered him that he smiled at her.

"I'm talking about your moving," he said. "What other reason could there be but some man?"

"You're crazy," she gasped, almost laughing as a wave of relief washed over her. He didn't know. He was so mad because he was jealous! Because he cared as much as she. "No. No man," she whispered, looking at him.

She didn't say the words, but he saw it in her eyes. "No. No man but you." With infinite tenderness, he pulled her to him. She buried her face against his chest, and he nuzzled the curls tickling his nose. "Then why?" he asked. "Why are you leaving me?"

"I'm not. Not yet."

"But soon?"

The head against his chest started to nod, switched to a negative movement, stopped. The whisper was so soft he had to strain to hear it. "I don't know. Maybe."

"Why?"

"Because," she said. And stopped. Because there was no way to undo what she had done, and she didn't want him to know. Because of people. Her mother, who would never condone the price Terri had paid for her life. Jasper Goodrich, to whom she owed all that money. And Mark, whom she loved. And who liked, maybe loved, Terri Thompson. She didn't want to see him change. Didn't want to see that look on his face, despising, condemning her.

"Why?" he again questioned.

"Don't ask."

He didn't ask. He didn't want to know. It no longer mattered who or what she was. What mattered was the pliant yielding of her soft body against his, setting his senses on fire, the sweetness drained from her lips, cascading through his veins in erotic waves of desire, her hungry response to the passionate urgings of his tenderly demanding touch.

All that mattered was that she was here, in his arms, and he never wanted to let her go.

CHAPTER ELEVEN

WHEN he was with her, nothing else mattered. But when he was away from her, the doubts surfaced. Was he a besotted fool so much in love that he didn't care what she was?

Or could he be mistaken? The state must be pretty thorough in checking credentials, and if she had come armed with a degree from Stanford and good recommendations...

The state had okayed Eric Saunders.

She had said nothing more about moving away, so maybe...

She had never said anything about it in the first place. It was Angie who spilled the beans. Angie, whom she had not wanted to leave in the lurch. Strange that a conniving woman would be scrupulous about not leaving a roommate holding the bag.

Still planning to move, though. He had confirmed with Angie that Terri was sending out applications all over the place. Applications for the same kind of job where she would commit the same kind of scam? Not likely. She'd be more apt to join her conspirator, wherever he was, for a different kind of scam.

I could be wrong about the whole thing. She might have no connection at all with Deedee Divine.

You want to believe you are mistaken because you are so bewitched by her you can't see straight. When her arms are around you, her lips pressed to yours... Damn. He became aroused just thinking about her.

Did she feel the same way about him? Her response was such that he couldn't believe she was putting on an act.

Always pulls away, doesn't she? At the crucial moment. Why?

Afraid fulfillment would mean commitment, and she is reluctant? Cautious?

Or because she's already committed to someone else and this is a practiced art she uses on suckers like you? Driving a man crazy till she gets what she wants.

What the hell could she want from me?

She's already got it, buddy. Four hundred thousand dollars. And she's still playing around just for the fun of it.

That thought cut him to the quick, and he refused to believe it. Terri was not a tease. She was an appealing woman and...

She had appealed to Robbie, all right. Had him so mesmerized he had defied his grandfather and planned to marry her.

If, damn it, she actually was Deedee Divine.

Robbie. He would know. Why hadn't he thought of that before? He had gone along, trusting his own judgment, which, God knows, was not reliable in this case. Robbie. He wouldn't say anything, just bring the two of them together. Sit back and see what happened.

There was a job opening in Dallas. They wanted her to come for an interview.

"Texas?" her mother said. "Why would you want to move there? Don't you like California?"

"The weather," she said. "It never changes."

"Well, it sure changes in Texas. Freezing in winter and hot as blazes in summer. Is that what you want? And what about your job? I thought you liked it."

She stopped arguing. She was running out of excuses. Lies.

Why did it have to be Mark Denton to whom she told that first awful—let's face it, monstrous lie?

Why did she have to fall in love with him? Totally, irrevocably, painfully in love. The flirtations, infatuations, mild involvements she had enjoyed with other men were as nothing compared to this. This never-before, never-will-it-come-again, deep-in-her-veins feeling of a joy so consuming, a passion so fulfilling that she wanted to grasp it, live it and never let it go.

She thought of her life without Mark, and the meaning of the poet's words became clear. "You will laugh, but not all of your laughter. You will cry, but not all of your tears."

How had he so quickly and completely enveloped her life? Thoughts of him filled all her wakeful moments and sleepless nights. He walked beside her even when she walked alone, smiled at her from the applications on her desk. And when she was in his arms, when he kissed her . . .

Sex. Her abstinence was not due entirely to moral principles. Never before had she wanted a man with every fiber of her being, never before so yearned to give and to take, to fully surrender to the exquisite primitive delight of joining, becoming part of another human being. Not until Mark. She loved him. She wanted him.

But each time, just as she was on the verge, like a neon sign they would flash before her. All those dollar signs, all four hundred thousand of them.

Like a brick wall, her lie stood between them.

Texas or Timbuctoo. She had to get away. And so she planned.

Yet, while she was near him, she was tempted to drain every moment of its pleasure. But when he suggested a weekend sail to Monterey to celebrate her birthday, she parried. "How did you know it was my birthday?"

"Angie told me."

"Angie has a big mouth."

"The better to hear things," he quipped. If it weren't for Angie, he'd be more in the dark than he already was. "So how about it?"

She hesitated. "I don't know." Alone with him on his boat. A whole weekend.

"Oh, come on. It'll be fun. Angie and her friend can't make it, but I invited another couple."

Another couple. No room for intimacy. And she'd be with Mark. "Sure. It does sound like fun."

There were predictions of a thunderstorm. But maybe not. At least the Saturday morning they were to set sail dawned bright and sunny, even warm. And it will get even warmer the further south we get, she reasoned as she donned white shorts and a matching top. She had told Mark she would walk across the park and meet him at the boat. Clutching her overnight case and the bag of fruit, cookies and other munchies she had gathered as a surprise, she started out.

However, halfway across the park, she stopped, intensely interested in the plight of three boys. Boys who, from their unkempt appearance, were not from this area. But often children from the crowded tenements some blocks away came here to fly their kites, one of which had become entangled in a tree. One boy was in the tree, trying to extract it. Another boy stood, holding onto the strings of two high-flying kites while calling directions to the boy in the tree. "Wait. Don't get on that branch. You'll tear it!"

The third boy, smaller than the other two, was watching, upset.

Terri dropped her parcels and sprang to the rescue. "I'll hold these," she said, seizing the strings of the flying kites. "You climb up and help. If you can pull that branch back while he..."

He gave a grateful nod and joined his companion in the tree. But when they brought the kite down, it was badly damaged and the small boy with red hair and a mass of freckles began to cry.

"Don't cry, Chip," said the boy who looked to be his brother. "Rusty'll make you another one."

Rusty, the first tree climber, nodded. "Sure I will."

Terri examined the kite, cleverly constructed from old newspapers and frail strips of balsam. Looked at Rusty, his very dark skin, keen features and very white teeth. "You made this?"

He nodded. "I could fix it if I had some paste and—"

"Wait," Terri said and retraced her steps.

When she looked up from the repaired kite, it was to see Mark gazing at her, an amused expression on his face.

"I lost track of time," she apologized, when he had picked up her overnight case and they were making their way to his boat.

"So I see."

"But I was fascinated. Did you see that kite Rusty made out of scraps and—"

"I saw it. I'm surprised you're not setting him up in business."

She grinned. "No need. He's done it himself. Fifteen cents a kite, he tells me. And I had some munchies for us. But I gave them all away."

"That doesn't surprise me," he said.

"It was just that Chip, the little boy, reminds me of the kid who lived next door to my aunt."

He smiled at her. "I bet everybody reminds you of someone. Even that old woman I bumped into the other day. You would probably have invited her to stop and have tea with you."

"What old woman?"

They had reached the boat by the time he had finished his amused recounting of the incident. She laughed. "Indeed I would not have invited her for tea. I—" She stopped as someone waved from the deck.

"Hi, Mark! We're here. Right on time."

Robbie. Oh, my God! Robbie Goodrich. For a moment, she was paralyzed by her own stupidity. Why had she never, not once, thought of this possibility? Robbie Goodrich had been completely erased from her mind.

But now... When he sees me... She wanted to run.

She couldn't run. Mark had her firmly by her hand and was pulling her onto the deck. "Come along. I want you to meet my nephew, Robbie Goodrich."

She couldn't look at him. She kept her eyes lowered, heard Mark say, "Robbie, this is my friend Terri Thompson." Waited for the explosion.

Heard Robbie's familiar voice, young and eager. "How do you do? I'm delighted to meet you." Calm. No surprise.

She opened her eyes. Robbie had hardly glanced at her. He was pulling his young companion forward. "Terri, did you say? Terri, this is Sue Allen."

Terri felt the world swing dizzily around her, right itself. With all the composure she could muster, she smiled, "Hello, Sue. And Robbie, is it?"

"Yeah. Golly! This is going to be great." He had turned away from her. "Mark, could we go on to San Simian? Sue has never seen Hearst Castle."

Mark answered that he didn't see why not, while Terri wondered that a wig could so completely hide her identity. Even from Robbie, who had seen much more of Deedee Divine than Mark had in only two encounters.

Even so, it was a full two hours before she could relax, feeling sure that he had no idea that he had seen her before. And was not particularly interested, more concerned with acting as Mark's copilot and answering the demands of his pretty blonde girlfriend. She was young and impressionable, explaining that she had never been on a private boat as large as this before and wasn't everything wonderful!

It was wonderful. An impressive trip Terri was to remember all the rest of her life. Sailing down the coastline of California, with its high rugged cliffs, inlets and sandy beaches, past redwood forests or cleared farmlands. Hearing occasional barks of sea lions. Once, to Sue and Terri's delight, they got close enough to one of the rocky islands to see the great sea creatures basking in the sun. "Looking like rocks themselves," Terri said, "until you see one move."

There were other boats, of course, but Terri felt they were enclosed in a companionable capsule of their own. Far away from other people and disturbing thoughts. The men manned the boat, the women cooked or fixed appetizing picnic lunches. They played rollicking, highly competitive games of Scrabble, poker and chess, sunned themselves on the deck and enjoyed the spectacular scenery.

They docked at Monterey, rented a car and toured the area, driving along Carmel's famous seventeen-mile drive. They visited the fish emporium, which Mark and Robbie had seen before and was not of much interest to Sue. But Terri was as excited as a child over all the sea urchins and an especially colorful star fish. They had quite a time getting her out of the museum.

That night they celebrated Terri's twenty-third birthday at a posh restaurant overlooking the ocean, dancing and a candlelight dinner, birthday cake and all. Quite a festive affair, shared by the other diners who joined in singing "Happy Birthday" and partook of the big birthday cake. Presents, as well. From Sue and Robbie, who had been alerted to the occasion, delicate figurines, replicas of the sea urchins with which she had been so enchanted. Terri was delighted.

And from Mark... Terri unwrapped the narrow package and opened the velvet case. A dainty, beautifully designed jeweled bracelet, a string of matching sapphires entwined and linked by tiny diamonds. Exquisite. A lump rose in her throat and she had trouble breathing.

"Here," said Mark, taking it from her. "Let me put it on. I couldn't resist. It suits you."

"Oh?" She looked at him, wanting to say more, how wonderful, beautiful, thank you. But her mouth felt dry and she couldn't speak.

"There," he said, fastening the catch. "Perfect. Matches your eyes. Sapphires, the same color, and diamonds with their sparkle."

She touched the bracelet tenderly, reverently, looked at Mark, holding back the tears. She couldn't keep it. It was worth a fortune. And she had already taken too much from him. She hoped he would never know. But if he did find out, she wanted him to remember that Terri Thompson was not as greedy and grasping as Deedee Divine.

It would break her heart, but she would return the bracelet. Later. Not now when he was looking so proud and pleased over the birthday he had given her.

"This is the most wonderful birthday of my life," she said, smiling at him.

He had watched closely and there had been no sign of recognition on Robbie's part, Mark thought, as he backed the boat from the wharf and headed for San Simian. Surely if she were Deedee Divine, Robbie would know it. Of course Robbie's love life was not too stable. Seemed to switch affection quite easily, from a belly dancer to a debate opponent named Debby on the east coast. Now he was enamored with Sue, this freshman from Berkeley. No, Robbie's emotions weren't altogether reliable.

But there as nothing wrong with his eyesight. And a different hairdo couldn't change a woman that much. If Terri was Deedee Divine, Robbie ought to know it. He was going to marry her. Ought to know her if he ever saw her again.

He doesn't know her. So maybe I'm wrong. Two different women.

Damn it, nothing wrong with my eyesight, either. And I'd swear!

I'm going to ask Robbie point-blank. First time I get him alone I'll ask if he sees any resemblance between—

Remember, you're not supposed to know this Divine woman.

Hell! Well, I'll figure it out. Find some way to bring it up.

Anyway, he mused with a wry chuckle, why am I mooning over this woman? Why don't I get this charade over? Ask the question and demand an answer. "Are you the crook I think you are, or aren't you?"

Ah! Therein lies the rub. I've become so emotionally involved I couldn't stand the wrong answer.

Meanwhile, on with the show. He was watching Terri as closely as he watched Robbie, and she didn't exhibit any signs of recognition, either. But he was sure she would be careful not to.

Neither does she exhibit any of the characteristics of a con lady, he decided later, as he observed her during the tour of Hearst Castle. She seemed more displeased than impressed by its opulence.

It was Sue who went bonkers over the grandeur. The guest houses furnished with fabulous antiques gathered from castles and grand houses all over the world, the Olympic-size swimming pool and the beautiful sculptures, the saints carved on the ceiling and the huge table in the refectory room, even the vast grounds of the menagerie and its few remaining animals. "Imagine!" she said. "Someone loving you enough to give you all these treasures!"

"Load you with all this junk, seems more like it," Terri said.

Sue didn't seem to hear her. "It's so grand. Wouldn't you love to live here?"

"No. I think it much more suitable as a museum." Seeing Sue's look of surprise, she shrugged. "Okay, I guess I don't have any taste," she concluded.

Certainly not the taste of a con woman, Mark thought. Not when she has more interest in

starfish and kites made of old newspapers than
these priceless treasures.

On the way up the coast, the promised storm
broke. There was some thunder and lightning and
the rain came down in torrents. The boat was
tossed and buffeted by the wind and waves,
sending objects flying to the floor. Mark and
Robbie maneuvered the boat to harbor, and Terri
tried to calm an almost hysterical Sue. The
heaving boat made her seasick and she retched,
making quite a mess.

Terri managed to clean up, and found the pills
for seasickness, so that by the time they docked,
Sue was calm. The two men got pretty drenched
tying up the boat and welcomed the hot coffee
and crisp toast Terri had prepared for them. They
waited out the storm with games and good
humor, and soon sailed swiftly to San Francisco.

Mark did not have to seek Robbie out. Robbie
sought him out, appearing at his flat early the
next morning.

"What's with the early bird act?" Mark asked
when, draped in a towel, shaving lather still on
his face, he opened the door.

"Wanted to catch you before you left for
work," Robbie answered.

"So you caught me. What's up?"

"Wanted to ask what you thought of Sue."
Robbie followed Mark back to the bathroom and
lounged in the doorway, watching him shave.

"Seems like a nice kid." Young, Mark thought. Not that it mattered. Given Robbie's rate, he'd soon move on. "Why? Serious?"

"Kinda. And that's just it. Remember Debbie? I told you about her. She was on that debating team, and we've been, well, keeping in touch. She's thinking of transferring here and if I'm tied up with Sue..."

"Easy, my boy. You've got to learn to play it cool. Don't get too serious too quick." He gave Robbie pointers on playing the we're-the-best-of-friends game, weighing the merits of one friend against another. He laid aside his shaving gear, splashed on some after-shave and seized upon the opening. "By the by, what do you think of Terri?"

"Real nice. I liked her." Robbie frowned. "You know, she kinda reminds me of someone."

"Oh?" Mark was instantly alert.

"Yeah. Remember that belly dancer I told you about?"

"Belly dancer?" Mark tried to speak casually, as if puzzled, but he could hardly get the words out.

"Maybe I didn't tell you. But she had me so turned on, I was all set to marry her."

"I see. And this, er, dancer reminds you of Terri? Looks like her?" Mark threw aside the towel and strode into the bedroom, as if he could care less.

"Heck, no. Doesn't look at all like her. Deedee, that was her name, had long black hair and blue eyes. Or were they gray?" Robbie rubbed his nose. "Can't remember. But she was, well, more curvy. And boy, could she wiggle that torso, swing her hips. Got to you, man. I could watch her all night."

Mark, listening keenly as he struggled into his pants, thought Robbie hadn't been in love with a woman at all. He had lusted after a provocative belly dancer. Yes, he remembered the feeling. . . .

"No," Robbie said. "It's not the way Terri looks that reminds me of Deedee. It's the way she acts. Did you see how she looked after Sue when she got sick on the boat?"

Mark nodded, his eyes never leaving Robbie's face as he put on his shirt.

"That's just the way Deedee looked after me when I was at her place. That night she—"

Mark paused in the act of buttoning his shirt, swallowed. "You stayed at her place some nights?"

"Oh, no. Just that one night. I got drunk, you see, and she said it wasn't safe for me to drive. So she took me home with her." He told about the hot coffee, sleeping on the sofa, the note she left the next morning, disappearing before he woke up. Their continuing friendship. "She didn't make me feel uncomfortable, you see. Just like Terri didn't make Sue uncomfortable. Deedee had that kind of knack. Even with those guys in the bar...some of them could be kinda crude, you know. But they all respected, liked her. Guess 'cause she seemed to like them. She had a kind of...well, I guess you'd call it grace about her. Terri has that kind of grace, too. I like her.''

CHAPTER TWELVE

MARK talked into his dictaphone, the words rolling off his tongue with their usual perspicacity. "The question—are the state and the nation really taking care of business? Preliminary evidence tends to say no. Hence, if multiplied by the fifty states, the small business agency would be, or is, a major player in the federal deficit increase. But, again, current findings are sketchy."

Mark stopped his dictation and thought, Am I soft pedaling this caper? No, came his answer.

He continued. "This could be an aberration."

He switched off the machine. Leaned back in his chair, for the moment, his thoughts wandering to her again. It was not just lust. Robbie did get to know Deedee Divine. A belly dancer with a big heart.

Doesn't remember how she looks, though.

I do. Same eyes. Same dimple. Same grace.

He sat up. Hmm, he mused. Some questions are just too damn hard to figure out. Like how does a woman of goodness and grace figure in a double-dealing con game.

The door opened and Ginger bounced across the floor. "'Scuse me, boss, but I thought you'd want to answer this right away."

He scanned the fax sheet she handed him. "Right. Take a letter."

Ginger sat beside him, notepad poised, when Brian burst in. "Got a funny feeling, boss."

Mark looked up and chuckled, seeing what he called Brian's J. Edgar Hoover expression. "Found a culprit, have you?"

"Right here in the city by the bay."

"Oh?"

"Yep. Saunders wasn't in this by himself."

For a second, Mark's motor system lurched. Damn! Not Terri, he hoped. "You have proof of this?"

"Not proof, exactly. Just a feeling in my bones. Complicity." He gave Mark a satisfied nod. "Good suggestion of yours, by the by, to have a talk with Saunders's wife."

"She gave you a lead?"

"Not she. He really did her in. She woke up one morning to find he had split with all the loot."

Ginger looked up from her notes and shook her head. "Umph! Umph! Umph! Now ain't that just like a man? To walk out and leave the woman holding the bag."

"Holding hot air," Brian said. "He took everything else."

"Dirty low down man."

"Damn fool woman, I'd say. To let some dude take you for all you've got in two short months."

"Con man," Ginger fumed. "And that's the way they work. Quickly."

Mark stared at her, his mind racing. He had been taken in in just a few short minutes. He cleared his throat, cutting into Brian's retort. No time for this sexist game. He had to know. "Complicity?" he asked, not wanting to hear the answer. Not wanting his suspicions confirmed.

Brian nodded. "Had to be. Nobody in his right mind would okay that much money for that kind of setup."

"Oh."

"Yeh. Thought I might as well have a look at the so-called plant while I was down there."

"And?"

"Fake all the way. Just a little carpentry shop left by the deceased father of the latest Mrs Saunders, used by her for her little ceramics hobby until it was converted by Saunders into a would-be pottery plant that wouldn't fool anybody who wasn't in on the take. Get it?"

Mark got it. And was sickened. The bank would not check on a loan guaranteed by the State, subjected to the careful scrutiny of an agency, dependent on a loan officer who—

"Of course I'm sure some official is already quietly checking into this, but you know how that works. If someone higher up is involved, the bones can be easily buried. So I thought I might nose around the agency and—"

"No. Wait!" At Brian's look of surprise he knew he had spoken too sharply. He forced himself to be casual. "I've got connections there.

I'll work from that end. You continue the search for Saunders.''

I must be crazy, he thought, as Brian gave his okay-you're-the-boss sign and went out. But he wished he hadn't set Brian on the trail. No matter. Obviously others were on the trail. And they would discover...

He didn't want that. Didn't want to expose her. Didn't want her exposed.

He finished the letter he was dictating, even managed to finish a first draft of his column. But his mind was elsewhere. Was he in love with a woman he couldn't like? No matter. He had to warn her. No, ask her, damn it! He could be wrong.

Whatever. It was time to stop cutting bait and fish. He had to confront her.

Time was running out.

Terri sat at the little desk in her bedroom and faced up to it. She had to make a decision. And she had to make it soon. Accept one of the new job offers. Leave the job she had.

That was the hard part. Leaving.

Spectacular things were happening in California's small business arena. People like Joe Daniels and Mary Ables were becoming independent for the first time in their lives. Not only independent and gainfully employed, but employing others. The Small Business Administration was indeed a launching pad for multimillion-dollar corporations. To wit—the snowshoe manufacturing concern that had been started on a small scale by two sisters and was now one of California's major industries.

Yes, she liked her job. Liked the invigorating task of helping to put into operation wonderful constructive new ideas. She thought of the applications waiting on her desk. There was one from Arnold Stokes, a Vietnam veteran, an amputee, who, sitting in his wheelchair, had devised a computer game for deaf children. How much the development of such games would mean, both to the children and to Stokes. She had to get this project launched before she left. She would show Mr Anderson that it would pay, she vowed, remembering her boss's warning. "The trouble with you, Terri, is you think in terms of people, instead of dollars and cents, which, I must remind you, is what business is all about."

But products designed for special people could be profitable, as well. Anyway, money is not all that business is about, she thought. It's also about people, people with ideas and ambition, People with dreams. Dreams waiting in the in basket on her office desk.

She sighed. Ah, well. People with dreams lived in Dallas too. And Albany.

Which should it be?

She lifted the two envelopes containing the best job opportunities, one in each hand, balancing them against each other, as if weight would determine her decision. She didn't need to open the envelopes again. She knew what they contained.

Texas, trying to recover from the worst economic slump in its history. New York, about to tumble into one. Both needing the kind of help she had been trained to give.

Expertise that her mother had paid for by dancing on stages or showrooms or dingy bars all across the country. Mom always pretended it was fun, Terri thought. Not until Spike's did I know the difficulties, the circumstances under which she worked to sell her one talent. But she never sold herself.

As I did.

Not that I regret it for one minute! When I see Mom, her brave and cheerful self, the bloom returning to her cheeks, I am glad I did it. Glad!

If only it hadn't been Mark. If only...

She opened the box containing the birthday bracelet, lifted it out. The jewels twinkled at her as her fingers reverently caressed the dainty chain. She longed to keep it...something of him to hold on to. She couldn't. It was too precious, too valuable. If he knew...

She wouldn't think about that now. She put the bracelet back, and resolutely shut the container.

Albany or Dallas, which? Albany would almost be like coming home. She and Mom would not be far from Aunt Meg and her cousins in New York City. But Mark Denton was often in New York, and though they'd probably never meet...

Dallas would be the better choice. A place most unlikely to hold any interest for Mark Denton.

*   *   *

"We'll have dinner at the yacht club," Mark had said over the phone. More private, but surrounded by other people. He could keep his senses and do some straight talking. He would be less inclined to take her into his arms and be lulled into insensibility by the intoxicating pressure of her body against his, soft and yielding.

Now, seated across from her at the club, he knew the place didn't matter. The invitation was still there in those alluring blue eyes, drawing him like a magnet, shutting out thought. He concentrated on the wine list, ordered. Then, still avoiding her eyes, he opted for straight talk. "So. You're still planning to leave town?"

"Yes."

"Why?"

Terri gave a little start. He had sounded so blunt, accusatory. "I—it's personal."

"Something to do with the scandal?"

"Scandal?" What was he talking about?

"That stunt pulled by Eric Saunders."

"Oh." She had to give him some reason. This was as good as any. "Yes. Partially. I do feel responsible."

So it was she. "You okayed the loan?"

"Yes." As chief loan officer, hers was the final go-ahead on all loans.

He was suddenly so angry he wanted to shake her. Shock her into realizing what she had done. "Why did you do it? Two hundred thousand dollars is a lot of money to shell out for a fake outfit. You must have known it was fake." He leaned forward, willing her to deny it. "It must have been as obvious to you then as it is obvious to investigators now!"

"It...well, I suppose—" She broke off, puzzled. Why the uproar about Saunders? They had hardly mentioned him before. Even at that conference—

"Well?" he barked. "Don't you agree that two hundred thousand was a pretty hefty bundle?"

"Yes," she faltered, staring at him. Seeing the fury in dark steely eyes that burned into hers. As they had that night at Spike's. And two hundred thousand was not nearly as much as four hundred thousand, she thought. If he knew... She shivered. "I know it was a mistake," she said. "But at the time, I was so busy that I..." Just signed anything, she thought, her voice trailing off, remembering how it had been. Working two jobs, back and forth to the hospital, frightened for Mom. "At the time, you see, I was so much involved."

Too involved to pull out, he thought. He softened. A young girl with that sweet, innocent-looking face, a girl with a soft heart...easy to be suckered into a con game by a practiced felon. "You are thinking of other activities that might be exposed?"

She nodded. No telling how many mistakes she had made during that critical period. "When someone you love is at risk," she said, "it...well, it just kind of blocks out everything else and I guess you don't always know what you're doing. You see..." She stopped, appalled at herself. She had been about to tell him everything. All about Mom, the dancing and the four hundred thousand dollars! She couldn't do that. She couldn't. He would never forgive her.

"Someone you love." That was the key. What was it Brian had said? "A ladies' man, quite an appeal to the ladies." Yes, Terri, who saw only good in everyone, would be vulnerable. If she fell in love...

Someone you love. That explained everything. Why, no matter the passion rampant between us, she always pulled away. She might not be a saint, but Terri was a true-blue kind of woman who would remain loyal to one man. Who would do anything for the man she loved.

And she had fallen in love with a con man who was using her. Ruining her life. If he could get his hands on that no good son of a—

The touch of her soft hand on his clenched fist startled him, and he looked up to see guilt and painful regret on her face. "Please. Don't be angry," she said. "It was a big blunder. No wonder you and the rest of the press are after the agency's blood and mine, but—"

"No. You're wrong. I don't know about the press, but I'm not after blood, particularly not yours." He realized as he said it that, without a doubt, it was true. All he wanted to do was... "I want to help you. If you'll let me," he said.

"Thank you. I hope you will speak out for the agency. And, since it was my fault, my leaving will make it easier to—"

"Don't go! Look, we'll work this out." Some way, somehow, he would get her out of this mess, he thought.

She shook her head, finding it hard to speak. Her eyes fastened upon his, hungrily absorbing the love...was it love that she saw there? Her heart pounded, her veins on fire, wanting, as everything within her reached out to him. If only... She looked away. "I have to go," she whispered. She couldn't bear to see that look change to hate.

"Why?"

"It's not just here, the—the scandal." She paused, swallowing the lump in her throat. "There's something else."

"Tell me."

"I can't. Maybe, in a new environment. In time, perhaps, when I've..." When I've paid my debt, she thought, her voice trailing off. Unable to face him, she kept her eyes down. Salad. When had the waiter placed it there? She couldn't swallow a thing. "I'm sorry," she said. "I...I'm not... Please take me home."

He saw the tears welling in her eyes. The panic. This was not the time to pressure her.

"Of course," he said, and signaled the waiter.

When he left her at her door, she slipped something into his pocket. He hardly noticed.

Later, when he took off his jacket, it slipped to the floor.

The bracelet. And a note. "Thank you for the thought, more valuable than the bracelet, which, because of certain circumstances, I cannot accept."

He read the note twice. Certain circumstances. A jealous boyfriend?

Too valuable?

That's a laugh. A four hundred thousand dollar con woman not accepting a two thousand dollar bracelet?

Didn't add up.

CHAPTER THIRTEEN

MARK paced the floor of his living room.

Didn't add up.

Still, she all but admitted she was in on the take.

All right. So she's not a saint.

Vulnerable? Easily influenced by someone she loves? At heart she's decent, honest. I see it in her face. The poem winged through his mind. "Sheds the lustre of purity, goodness and grace...carries her loveliness stamped on her face."

That's what's got you, buddy, that face.

Yeah. He shook his head, but couldn't shake off her image. He was hooked. Like some damn fool sophomore.

He walked over to the bar. Poured himself a drink. Sipped it slowly.

Okay, she's got me! He set the glass down hard.

But I'm not exactly a fool. I read character pretty good. Terri Thompson hasn't the character of a con woman. Doesn't like to hurt people.

Didn't bat an eye when she took your four hundred thousand dollar check, did she?

He looked down at the bracelet. It just didn't add up. If he could get to the bottom line...

He picked up the phone.

* * *

Terri had gone to bed, but she couldn't sleep. She lay awake, wishing she could shut out the thoughts spinning through her brain.

When the phone rang, her first thought was Mom, and she hurriedly reached for it. "Hello?"

"Terri?"

"Yes." she hugged the phone. He had called. He wasn't angry that she had left so abruptly.

"Listen, we need to talk."

"No, please, I..." Her voice trailed off. There were things she was not yet ready to share.

"All right. We won't talk. We'll just...just take a drive."

"A drive? Where?"

"Nowhere. Anywhere. We'll just follow the highway. Wouldn't you like that?"

"Oh. Oh, yes!" She would like it. Alone with Mark. Just driving. Going nowhere. Thinking nothing.

"Good. Tomorrow. I'll pick you up at seven. We'll take the whole day."

"But I have to work."

"You know what they say about all work and no play. You do have some leave time, don't you?"

"Yes, but..." She thought of the applications on her desk. Things she had to complete before she left.

"And since you're planning to leave soon..."

And never see him again. Her heart gave a painful lurch. Just to be with him, a whole day.

Going nowhere. Not worrying about the past,
Not pondering the future. Just—

"Terri, are you there?"

"Yes. And, oh, yes! I'd love it. I'll be ready."

It was not true that he had no destination. He
would head unerringly toward the town of
Watsonville, location of the ill-fated Saunders
Pottery Plant. Where the woman Saunders had
left behind still lived.

"A woman whose life was destroyed in two
short months," Brian had declared. "Tough just
talking to her. Like to bust out crying myself."

If Terri, who didn't like to see people hurt,
could see her... If her eyes could be opened to
the hurt and havoc left in the wake of con
games...

He did not like being devious and did not
expect to enjoy the drive.

He reckoned without Terri's determination to
extract every ounce of joy from each last moment
she would ever spend with Mark. Moments to be
held and cherished for the rest of her life.

There was no trace of last night's trauma in
the face that greeted him that morning. Her smile
was warm, her eyes radiant with anticipation and
joy. She wore pale green slacks and top, a
matching jacket slung over her shoulder. She
looked fresh and young and innocent. He wanted
to wrap his arms around her and keep her just
like that. He swallowed, looked down at the
basket in her hand.

"What's all this?"

Her smile widened as she handed him the picnic basket. "We don't want to run out of sustenance as we venture into the wilderness, do we?"

Wilderness, indeed. He thought of all the traffic and eateries that cluttered the highway all the way to Watsonville, and flushed with guilt.

"Let's take Highway One," she said. "It's about as nowhere as you can get. And all those vista points, nothing but sky and cliffs and ocean."

She looked so happy and expectant that his heart turned over. Well, it would take longer, but Highway One also headed toward Watsonville.

It was the same route they had taken on the boat ride to Monterey, only from the shore this time. Winding around the coastal range, around dizzying curves, high cliffs on one side and a steep descent to the ocean on the other. Very little traffic, thank God. And from this side, too, one of the most spectacular views in the world.

She had planned well. At the first vista point, they had crescent rolls and coffee from a well filled thermos. She had brought her camera, and with wild delight was snapping pictures. Her enthusiasm was contagious as she pointed the lens from one place to another. "Oh, look, Mark, isn't that beautiful? Do you think I can catch those seals on that island? Stand right there so I can get you in this one."

"Your coffee is getting cold," he warned her. "Here, take a drink. And then stand right there where I can snap you."

"Oh, yes, I'd like to have one of me, as well."

No, this one's for me, he thought, seeing her framed against the sky, her curls tousled by the wind, face flushed, eyes glowing with happiness. Couldn't he keep her that way?

When they returned to the car, he wondered again just how involved she was with Saunders, what it would take to unravel the mess, detach her from him. Would she want to be detached?

He made another try. "Terri, you like your job. Must you go? Perhaps there is a way—"

"Mark, you promised."

"Okay." He switched to safer topics. The weather, a column he was writing, a loan application she wondered about. But he was more determined that she see Saunders's latest ex.

When they stopped for lunch, the sun was high, glinting on the steep rocky cliffs, the ocean far below and a distant tiny island. Wrapped in its golden glow, basking in its warmth, they stood together, awed by the magnificence and beauty.

"It's like being on top of the world, isn't it?" Terri whispered. "And you feel so alive, and so much at peace, as if you're part of it all. And you know without a doubt that someone up there is in charge of everything, the trees, the cliffs, the ocean...and you. And all your petty concerns are...petty. Maybe that's why some people become hermits, huh? Just take off and leave the mundane world behind." She stopped. "I'm being silly, aren't I?"

"No. Not silly. Terri, will you marry me?"

"What?" His words spun through her, an electric current of joy, apprehension and dread. She reeled from the shock. She couldn't believe he wasn't touching her, so strong was the passion between them. Couldn't believe he had said... "What did you say?"

"I asked you to marry me." He couldn't believe it. Whatever she had done, whoever she was. He wanted her.

"I—there's something—" She almost felt she could tell him. There was such love, such gentleness, such compassion in the dark eyes staring at her. Such adoration. A tremor of fear ran through her. Neither sun nor mountains nor someone up there could erase a lie and four hundred thousand dollars. "Time," she said. "I must have time." Time to gather courage.

"I'll wait," he said.

Another car drove into the rest area, breaking the spell. A rather beat up Volkswagen, out of which came a young couple who looked to be barely out of their teens. The girl was rosy, plump and quite pregnant. The boy was redheaded and freckled. A jolly, likable couple who were as awed by the view as they. They also had a camera, and the two couples were soon snapping pictures of each other. For the first time, Terri and Mark stood together for a picture.

Terri had brought paper cups and the couple shared the wine and sandwiches she had packed.

"Only one glass of wine for each of us," she said. "We need all of our faculties going around this mountain."

Still munching on fruit and cookies, they continued the drive in companionable silence, each wrestling with their own private thoughts. Mark, determined to force the issue and concerned about how to deal with the can of worms he was sure to open. Terri, wanting, but afraid to confide.

"Watsonville," Mark said, when they reached the town. "Isn't that where Eric Saunders set up that fake pottery plant?"

"Yes, it is." She sat up, alert, and surprised him by saying, "I'd like to take a look at that."

Just as if she had never seen it before, he thought, but did not say it.

They found it without too much trouble. It was a small two-story building, and was tightly closed. Terri peered through a wide dirty window while Mark knocked loudly on the door. Brian had told him the woman lived in an upstairs room. Eventually she appeared, a small woman in baggy jeans and a paint-smeared pullover. Thin blonde hair touched with gray hung limply to her shoulders, and her pale blue eyes were dull and lifeless.

"You're Mrs Saun—" Mark broke off as her nostrils twitched and she gave an emphatic shake of her head.

"Jane Boyers," she said. "What do you want?"

"This is Terri Thompson from the Small Business Administration, and we'd like to talk with you if we could."

"I'm talked out," she said. "Told everybody everything I know."

This woman has been through enough, Mark thought, and maybe he was being cruel, using her just to show Terri the plight in which she had been left. It was Terri who spoke.

"No questions," she said. "We're not here to bother you. But I am curious about the plant. Could we please have a look?"

The woman shrugged. "If you like, what's left of it," she said, opening the door to admit them into a disheveled front room, evidently originally the display room. A few ceramic pots and figurines remained on some shelves, while broken bits of clay, paper and containers littered the floor.

Jane Boyers apologized. "I've been meaning to clean up. Just haven't had much energy lately." But she willingly led them through the rest of the plant, consisting of one small kiln, a pottery wheel, bottles of glazes, a few casks containing clay, brushes, things one would use in a small hobby shop. "Which was what it was until I met Eric," Jane explained. "He rented big kilns and other equipment and had everything looking real good until... Well you know." She seemed to warm to Terri, who was interested and sympathetic, and soon poured out the whole story.

A lonely woman who had been wooed and won by Eric Saunders. She gave him all she had. She cashed out her retirement, withdrew her small savings, sold her house. "To start this business, you see," she finished through tears. "And, well, you see what it came to. He took all I had."

Just like Brian, Mark was impressed, almost in tears himself. At least he had accomplished what he had set out to do. There was no way Terri could fail to recognize the destruction, the harm perpetrated through such a heist.

Strangely, Terri didn't look at all guilty. Sympathetic, yes. But more...interested? She had turned from the woman and was examining a small figurine, a girl playing a flute. "This is your handiwork?" she asked Jane.

The woman nodded.

"And this?" Terri ran her hand gently over the figure of a swan.

Again Jane nodded.

Terri turned a beaming face to her. "Oh, you're wrong, Jane Boyers. Eric Saunders did not take all you had. Don't you know what an unusual talent you have?" Mark watched in amazement as Terri touched, admired, praised. And, as she talked, he saw Jane Boyer's eyes light up.

"Oh, yes," said Terri. "You still have what you had when Eric Saunders met you. What you have to do is use it for yourself." Terri took pad and pen out of her purse and began to figure. This building was in the hands of the receivers, but hard to sell, and might easily be leased. Jane's living quarters were already upstairs. She could convert the downstairs into a hobby and sales shop. "This is a tourist community, art lovers and souvenir seekers all over the place, and your exquisite figurines..." She talked of a hobby shop and training classes for amateurs. "You have most of the equipment you need. You might be able to arrange a small loan through the agency."

Mark watched, fascinated. This was Terri at work. This was a woman who had the interest, personality and insight as well as training for her chosen field. A woman far too smart to get caught in a shell game. Certainly there was no trace in her behavior that would indicate complicity with Saunders. No hint, verbal or otherwise.

All that this trip had accomplished was to pull a mistreated woman out of her depression and get her going again. In a big way, he thought, as he saw vigor return to Jane Boyers's face, saw her come alive with purpose. Looking at Terri's curly head bent over her pad, dealing with facts and figures, he felt a surge of pride.

Something else had been accomplished by this trip. He was more in love. More confused.

What now?

As sure as my name is Mark Denton, this woman is Deedee Divine.

Isn't she?

but him, to sell, and might easily be fixed. Looking at herself in the shop's full-length mirror, she could
picture the room, fitting into Clifford's study and some-

CHAPTER FOURTEEN

WHEN he got to his office the next morning the
news had broken. Eric Saunders had been picked
up in Chicago. In California the next day, he was
already plea bargaining, and named his accomplice, a former loan officer, James Turner.
Turner left the agency right after the Saunders
loan was processed.

"I couldn't believe it," Terri said when Mark
phoned her. "He was such a nice man. And he
resigned suddenly because he wanted to join his
mother who was ill in...in Canada, I think."

"A handy excuse," he said.

"Yes, I suppose so. But he seemed so concerned about her, his mother, I mean. And he
appeared so honest and straightforward. I can't
believe he would do such a thing."

Mark winced. He had believed it of her.

"Never mind," he said. "It's a great lead for
the column I'm going to write." Already written
in his mind. Eric Saunders, clearly a disgrace.
But one fraudulent act measured against an
otherwise excellent record must not be allowed
to damage the agency. The small business arena
was a major player in building the economy of
the nation, as well as the state. He would cite
examples highlighting the activities of California's
Small Business Administration, praising the work

of the agency, and particularly the expertise of
its chief loan officer, Terri Thompson, who ex-
amines people as carefully as she does their businesses, and has been known to take risks that
have paid off for the State as well as the persons
concerned. Not much payback for the accusations he had harbored against her.

"Terri," he said, "I love you."

"Mark. Oh, Mark..." A soft murmur, en-
veloping his name with love, but also a cry of
anguish. "I, too. I do love you Mark. I do."

Relief. Pleasure. But what was the problem?
"Terri, you've had time."

"I know."

"Tonight," he said firmly. "I'll be over right
after work."

Terri's hand lingered on the phone after she
replaced it. Tonight. She shrank from the ordeal.

He loves you. He said so. He asked you to
marry him. You ought to be able to tell him
anything.

Oh, yeah? "Look, I have to explain. I'm not
who you think I am. Well, yes, I am, but... You
see I first met you as a belly dancer in a joint
called Spike's. And you thought—that is, I let
you believe...

God! A lie is a lie is a lie and four hundred
thousand dollars is a monstrous sum of money.
And I don't owe it to him. I owe it to that stern-
faced old man who was at his mother's that night,
and kept firing all those questions at me. Like
he was looking me over with a spyglass and wondering why Mark brought me without first con-

sulting him. And that was when I was being perfectly polite and respectable. If he knew...

Forget him. It's Mark who loves you.

Loves Terri Thompson. Not Deedee Divine.

Tell him. Your mother was ill and you needed...

Sure, play on his sympathies, grovel and—

"Miss Thompson," said the clerk who entered her office after a preliminary knock, "a man from the district attorney's office is here, asking to see the Saunders file. Shall I bring him in?"

"Of course. And bring me the Saunders file," she said, her mind focusing on the case. How could Turner get the agency in such a mess? She could see him now... "I know you're short-handed, and I hate to leave on such a short notice, but my mother, you see. She is ill and..."

The same explanation she would give to Mark tonight. But it wasn't a lie, not that part, at least. She shouldn't feel guilty. Ashamed. But she did. "Oh, good afternoon," she said to the man who was shown into her office. "Do have a seat." She pushed her own affairs to the back of her mind and went to work for the agency.

Mark left the office early that afternoon and went directly to the condo. The door was open and he walked into the living room to find Angie seated cross-legged on the floor, back straight, hands folded. Meditating?

No. Her eyes were open and she was grinning like crazy. And talking! "Thank you. Thank you. I know we will work well together."

He followed her gaze, trying to see to whom she spoke.

Nobody. Nothing.

He turned back to her. "What the hell are you doing?"

"Oh, Mark!" she snapped, and came out of whatever trance she was in. "You spoiled it."

"Spoiled what?"

"My visualization."

"Oh."

"It was going so well, too. Everybody was congratulating me, and telling me what a great job I was going to do, and I was just being modest and gracious, you know, just like Terri. And Mr Anderson came into Terri's office—my office, I mean—and he was saying, 'I'm delighted you're taking Terri's job. I know you will—'"

"Wait! Back up. What do you mean, you're taking Terri's job?"

"When she leaves, I mean."

"She isn't going anywhere." He would see to that.

"She certainly is. I don't have to visualize that. She's already given notice."

"She's taking it right back. I tell you, she's staying here."

Angie looked at him with disgust. "Mark Denton, you know very well she's taken that job in Dallas and will be leaving here in two weeks. And I'll be sitting in her office. That is, if you will kindly refrain from interrupting me when I'm visualizing myself in that position, being congratulated and—"

"Stop it! I tell you she's not going anywhere." He was suddenly furious. He wasn't sure what Terri was going to do. He took it out on Angie. "So you can just stop dreaming. That stupid stuff doesn't work, anyway."

"It certainly does work. Didn't I visualize myself in this very setting, over and over again, until Marge got in a bind and handed her condo to me, furniture and all, just like that!" Angie snapped her fingers. She stood up and waved her arms around the room. "You see me here, don't you? And then I visualized the perfect roommate and got Terri. And Terri. Do you know what Terri did? She visualized four hundred thousand dollars falling into her lap, just like I told her to do. And guess what! In two days it did! Four hundred thousand dollars! What do you think of that, Mr Know-it-all?"

He couldn't think. Couldn't speak. Could only stare at her, dumbfounded.

"Oho, that got your attention, didn't it? Four hundred thousand dollars. Right in her lap."

He found his voice. "Angie, does Terri dance? Professionally, I mean. Part time, maybe?"

Her look of surprise was genuine. "No, she doesn't do any part-time work. She's got a heavy-duty job. You know that."

No. Angie was wrong. She did dance professionally. At least she had some time back. As Deedee Divine. A belly dancer who had taken him for four hundred thousand dollars. His mouth twisted with derision, and he spat the words out, "Oh, she did something. Money doesn't fall into one's lap!"

"Oh, but it did into Terri's. Some old flake... No, he wasn't a flake. A good old benevolent soul, one of these do-gooders. What was his name? James, no Jasper Goodrich. He let her have the money, and she didn't even know him."

"Oh? And where did she meet this benevolent fool?"

"At the hospital, I think. He heard of her plight and loaned her what she needed. She's paying him back."

Right. According to Nate, regular monthly checks of one hundred dollars. He frowned, his eyes narrowing. Hospital? "What plight was she in?" he asked.

"Not her. It was her mother." He finally got the story, what she knew of it. How many people in the world would have that kind of money for a bone marrow transplant? But she had told Terri to just visualize it and, like a miracle, there it was! No, she was quite sure Terri had never danced professionally. Oh, her mother was a dancer, but back in New York, she thought. She had come out here to see Terri and collapsed. Isn't it strange how you can suddenly get dangerously ill, just like that? Terri was devastated.

"Where is Terri now?" he asked. He was itching to get his hands on her. To let him think what he had been thinking these past months!

"She's still at work. Big to-do about that Saunders thing, you know. You can wait for her. I'm on my way to my Life, Love, Living group."

"Go ahead," he said. "I'll wait."

It was almost eight when he heard her key in the lock. He stood up as she came into the living room.

"I'm sorry I'm late," she said, dropping her purse on the coffee table. "I called you and they said you had left."

"Left early," he said, keeping his voice level. "Anxious. Thought it was about time for some straight talk."

"Yes." Abruptly she turned, going toward the kitchen. "I'll make us some coffee." He followed her, stood against the doorjamb and watched her fumble nervously for the coffeepot, the canister. "Are you hungry? I could make some sandwiches," she said.

"I'm not hungry."

Still avoiding his eyes, she scooped up coffee grounds, filled the pot with water and talked rapidly. "Sorry to be late. Everything in turmoil, you know. The district attorney wanted to go over the records of Turner as well as Saunders. He was the loan officer who helped Saunders rip off the agency."

"Two hundred thousand, wasn't it?"

"Yes."

"Just half of what a belly dancer named Deedee Divine bilked from me."

She cut off the water faucet, turned. Carefully set the pot on the counter. Looked at him. "You know."

"Did you think you could hide your face under a wig?"

"But you didn't ... you acted as if you didn't. And Robbie ... he didn't know me."

"Robbie's not in love with you."

"Love? Don't you speak to me of love, Mark Denton." Her breathing was short and the words came haltingly. "You knew. From that very first night on the boat. All these months, and you never told me. Why?"

"I was waiting for you to tell me."

"Waiting for me to tell you? Playing this cat-and-mouse game, you mean. Torturing me while I—"

"Torture!" He stood up straight and looked down at her. "Do you know what kind of hell I went through, thinking you were mixed up with Saunders and wondering—?"

She stood away from the counter, her eyes blazing. "How could you? How could you think I'd abuse my position? Cheat the agency, defraud the people I had promised to serve?"

"Why not? You bilked me out of four hundred thousand dollars, didn't you?"

"But that isn't—wasn't..." She lifted her head, her eyes burning. "All right. But I was desperate. I really needed that money and when you walked in waving a bundle before me, what was I to do? Turn it down when my mother—" She broke off, the fire seeming to go out of her. "It was wrong of me," she said, looking so distraught that he softened.

He walked over and took her in his arms. "Sweetheart, you should have told me."

She pushed away. "Told you? I didn't even know you. Until there you were, staring down your nose at me, ready to shell out a bundle to rescue one of the precious Goodrich heirs from the clutches of a conniving bitch! Me."

He reached for her. "If you had explained the situation—"

"Explained? You already had me labeled a lying, cheating gold digger."

He couldn't help smiling. "I must say you played the part to perfection."

"Well, what would you have thought if I had told you I was really a nice girl, just filling in for my mother to help pay hospital bills, but it wasn't enough. And please would you lend me a half million bucks."

Now he laughed outright. "Okay. I suppose I would have been a bit skeptical. I did feel a bit of a fool after Robbie told me there were no marriage plans. But I'm glad you got the money." He looked suddenly serious. "How is your mother?"

"Wonderful! The transplant saved her life. She's getting stronger every day, and Mark, I am going to pay that money back to your uncle."

"Never mind. I've already paid him."

"You did? What did you tell him?"

"That the belly dancer admitted she lied, and I forced her to return the money."

"So I owe you?"

"Yes." He pulled her to him, buried his face in her curls. "All your love for all your life."

She nuzzled against his chest, her arms tight around his waist. "I do love you so much. It's such a relief, having it out at last."

"It is, indeed. Now, could we make plans? For a wedding, I mean?"

"Yes, only..." She looked at him, her eyes wary. "My mother doesn't know about the money. How I got it. If she ever meets Jasper Goodrich, she'll start thanking him and he'll find out."

"And think it a clever joke at my expense!"

"A joke!" She was appalled. "Four hundred thousand dollars! Anyway, Mom wouldn't... She would never forgive me for deceiving you and her and Mr Goodrich and..."

"Hush," he said. "Uncle Jasper hasn't a clue concerning his charities. I can fix that with Nate. Nate is the only one who knows what happened between Mark Denton and Deedee Divine. And he doesn't know anything about Terri Thompson. The real secret is ours alone. I promise to keep it."

"Thank you." She snuggled closer. "Oh, Mark, isn't it strange how terrible happenings can sometimes turn out terrific?"

"Oh?"

"Like I thought the end of the world had come when Mom got sick, but she's okay now. And if I hadn't danced at Spike's to pay the hospital bills and met Robbie, and you hadn't come and been so pompous and rude and— Oh, you know what I mean!''

He grinned. ''I think I get the message. Are you telling me you're lucky to be marrying a pompous, rude—?''

''Loving, intelligent, handsome, compassionate, forgiving, understanding, most wonderful man in the entire world. I do love you. It scares me to think I might not have found you except for what happened.''

''Scares me, too, love.'' He thought of the last line in his mother's poem—Wanted—a woman whose sweetness and graciousness fit like a gown...Do you think I might find such a one in this town?

He had found her.

* * * * *

Wednesday's child is full of woe...
Look out next month for Patricia Wilson's
heartwarming *Coming Home*, the latest book in
our exciting series.

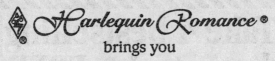

Harlequin Romance ®

brings you

How the West Was Wooed!

We've rounded up twelve of our most popular authors, and the result is a whole year of romance, Western style. Every month we'll be bringing you a spirited, independent woman whose heart is about to be lassoed by a rugged, handsome, one-hundred-percent cowboy! Watch for...

- July: **A RANCH, A RING AND EVERYTHING**—Val Daniels

- August: **TEMPORARY TEXAN**—Heather Allison

- September: **SOMETHING OLD, SOMETHING NEW**— Catherine Leigh

- October: **WYOMING WEDDING**—Barbara McMahon

Available wherever Harlequin books are sold.

Take 4 bestselling love stories FREE

Plus get a FREE surprise gift!

Special Limited-time Offer

Mail to Harlequin Reader Service®

3010 Walden Avenue
P.O. Box 1867
Buffalo, N.Y. 14240-1867

YES! Please send me 4 free Harlequin Romance® novels and my free surprise gift. Then send me 6 brand-new novels every month, which I will receive months before they appear in bookstores. Bill me at the low price of $2.67 each plus 25¢ delivery and applicable sales tax if any*. That's the complete price and a savings of over 10% off the cover prices—quite a bargain! I understand that accepting the books and gift places me under no obligation ever to buy any books. I can always return a shipment and cancel at any time. Even if I never buy another book from Harlequin, the 4 free books and the surprise gift are mine to keep forever.

116 BPA A3UK

Name	(PLEASE PRINT)	
Address		Apt. No.
City	State	Zip

This offer is limited to one order per household and not valid to present Harlequin Romance® subscribers. *Terms and prices are subject to change without notice. Sales tax applicable in N.Y.

UROM-696 ©1990 Harlequin Enterprises Limited

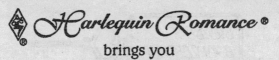

Harlequin Romance ®

brings you

Some men are worth waiting for!

Every month for a whole year Harlequin Romance will be bringing you some of the world's most eligible bachelors in our special **Holding Out for a Hero** miniseries. They're handsome, they're charming but, best of all, they're single! Twelve lucky women are about to discover that finding Mr. Right is not a problem—it's holding on to him!

Watch for:

#3415 THE BACHELOR'S WEDDING
by Betty Neels

Available wherever Harlequin books are sold.

UNLOCK THE DOOR TO GREAT ROMANCE
AT BRIDE'S BAY RESORT

Join Harlequin's new across-the-lines series, set in an exclusive hotel on an island off the coast of South Carolina.

Seven of your favorite authors will bring you exciting stories about fascinating heroes and heroines discovering love at Bride's Bay Resort.

Look for these fabulous stories coming to a store near you beginning in January 1996.

Harlequin American Romance #613 in January
Matchmaking Baby by Cathy Gillen Thacker

Harlequin Presents #1794 in February
Indiscretions by Robyn Donald

Harlequin Intrigue #362 in March
Love and Lies by Dawn Stewardson

Harlequin Romance #3404 in April
Make Believe Engagement by Day Leclaire

Harlequin Temptation #588 in May
Stranger in the Night by Roseanne Williams

Harlequin Superromance #695 in June
Married to a Stranger by Connie Bennett

Harlequin Historicals #324 in July
Dulcie's Gift by Ruth Langan

Visit Bride's Bay Resort each month wherever Harlequin books are sold.

BBAYG

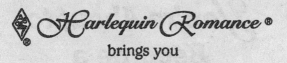

Harlequin Romance ®

brings you

Jessica Steele's

#3416 *A Wife in Waiting*

The heartwarming sequel to her November 1995 book, *The Sister Secret*.

Belvia and Josy Fereday are twins. Although they look alike, they're chalk and cheese when it comes to their characters.

Now that Belvia (the heroine of *The Sister Secret*) is happily married, the last thing Josy wants to do is intrude on her newlywed twin. Then Dacre Banchereau offers her an ideal solution—a home, a job and...marriage! But that's one proposal she wouldn't dream of accepting. Widowed and wary, Josy has decided that she just isn't marriage material. But Dacre Banchereau is a patient man. Is it only a matter of time before his wife in waiting becomes a bride in his arms?

Of *The Sister Secret:*

"Ms. Steele pens a touching love story with vivid characterizations, gripping scenes and a powerful conflict."
—*Romantic Times*

You're About to Become a Privileged Woman

Reap the rewards of fabulous free gifts and benefits with proofs-of-purchase from Harlequin and Silhouette books

Pages & Privileges™

It's our way of thanking you for buying our books at your favorite retail stores.

PROOF OF PURCHASE
HR-PP142
Offer expires October 31, 1996

Pages & Privileges™

Harlequin and Silhouette—
the most privileged readers in the world!

For more information about Harlequin and Silhouette's PAGES & PRIVILEGES program call the Pages & Privileges Benefits Desk: 1-503-794-2499

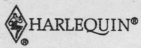

HARLEQUIN®

HR-PP142